William Shakespeare's Pericles, Prince of Tyre: A Retelling in Prose

David Bruce

Published by David Bruce, 2022.

WILLIAM SHAKESPEARE'S PERICLES, PRINCE OF TYRE: A RETELLING IN PROSE

First edition. July 28, 2022.

Copyright © 2022 David Bruce.

ISBN: 979-8201351144

Written by David Bruce.

Table of Contents

Dedication

DEDICATED TO MY SISTER MARTHA

Martha wrote, "When I was working at Longaberger, I worked with a girl who had two children and was in the middle of a divorce. She was so worried about Christmas for her boys. I received a very nice Christmas bonus that year, and I went to my boss and started a donation fund for the girl. My boss told me later that she — my boss —delivered the money to the girl's mother and father and told them not to tell her who brought the money for her. Months later the girl told me that the boys had the best Christmas that year, and she told me someone had brought money to her mom and dad for her, and she went to town and bought the boys Christmas. She never did know who did that for her. She was so thankful. I believe that I was the only one who donated to her, which was just fine."

***

The doing of good deeds is important. As a free person, you can choose to live your life as a good person or as a bad person. To be a good person, do good deeds. To be a bad person, do bad deeds. If you do good deeds, you will become good. If you do bad deeds, you will become bad. To become the person you want to be, act as if you already are that kind of person. Each of us chooses what kind of person we will become. To become a good person, do the things a good person does. To become a bad person, do the things a bad person does. The opportunity to take action to become the kind of person you want to be is yours.

Educate Yourself
Read Like A Wolf Eats
Be Excellent to Each Other
Books Then, Books Now, Books Forever

***

In this retelling, as in all my retellings, I have tried to make the work of literature accessible to modern readers who may lack the knowledge about mythology, religion, and history that the literary work's contemporary audience had.

Do you know a language other than English? If you do, I give you permission to translate this book, copyright your translation, publish or self-publish it, and keep all the royalties for yourself. (Do give me credit, of course, for the original retelling.)

I would like to see my retellings of classic literature used in schools, so I give permission to the country of Finland (and all other countries) to give copies of this book to all students forever. I also give permission to the state of Texas (and all other states) to give copies of this book to all students forever. I also give permission to all teachers to give copies of this book to all students forever.

Teachers need not actually teach my retellings. Teachers are welcome to give students copies of my eBooks as background material. For example, if they are teaching Homer's *Iliad* and *Odyssey*, teachers are welcome to give students copies of my *Virgil's* Aeneid: *A Retelling in Prose* and tell students, "Here's another ancient epic you may want to read in your spare time."

CAST OF CHARACTERS

Male Characters

ANTIOCHUS, King of Antioch. He is a widower.

PERICLES, Prince of Tyre.

HELICANUS and ESCANES, two Lords of Tyre.

SIMONIDES, King of Pentapolis.

CLEON, Governor of Tarsus.

LYSIMACHUS, Governor of Mitylene.

CERIMON, a Lord of Ephesus.

THALIARD, a Lord of Antioch.

PHILEMON, Servant to Cerimon.

LEONINE, Servant to Dionyza.

Marshal.

A Pandar.

BOULT, Servant to Pandar and Bawd.

Female Characters

The Daughter of Antiochus.

DIONYZA, Wife to Cleon.

THAISA, Daughter to Simonides.

MARINA, Daughter to Pericles and Thaisa.

LYCHORIDA, Nurse to Marina.

A Bawd.

Minor Characters

Lords, Ladies, Knights, Gentlemen, Sailors, Pirates, Fishermen, and Messengers.

DIANA.

JOHN GOWER, as Chorus.

SCENE. — *Various Mediterranean Countries.*

CHAPTER 1
— Prologue —

Addressing you the reader, John Gower, a resurrected 14th-century contemporary of Geoffrey Chaucer, and a poet who wrote on the topic of Pericles, said, "To tell a tale that was told of old, I, ancient John Gower, from ashes have come. I have taken for myself a human body and again taken on man's infirmities so that I can gladden your ears and please your eyes.

"What you are about to hear has been sung at festivals, and on ember-eves and holy-ales."

Embers are three-day periods of religious fasting. Often, people would enjoy themselves on the eve of an ember. A holy-ale was a happy religious festival.

Gower continued, "And lords and ladies in their lives have read this tale, which has appeared in many books, because of its restorative power — this feel-good tale is medicine for the reader. The benefit of reading this tale is to make men glorious. *Et bonum quo antiquius, eo melius.* Translation: And the older a good thing is, the better it is.

"If you, born in these latter times — later than my times — when learning is more sophisticated, accept my words and occasional rhymes, and if to hear an old man may bring pleasure to you, I would wish for life, so that I might spend it for you, like a burning candle that is spent as it gives light.

"Know that this location is Antioch. Antiochus the Great built up this city to be his chiefest seat, his capital. This city is the fairest in all Syria. I tell you now what I have learned from my authorities. This King took for himself a peer — a wife — who died and left a female heir, who was so lively, carefree, and beautiful of face that it was as if Heaven had lent her all his grace. The father, Antiochus, took a liking to her and provoked her to commit incest. Bad child; worse father! The father enticed his own daughter to do evil that should be done by none. But with time the incest they committed began to seem no sin to them — when one is accustomed to sin, the sin seems to be no sin.

"The beauty of this sinful dame made many Princes go to her, to seek her as a wife and bedfellow, and make her in marriage-pleasures his playfellow.

"To prevent her marrying one of her suitors, Antiochus made a law to keep her always with him and to keep men in awe so that they would not seek to wed her. The law stated that whoever asked her to be his wife must find the answer to a riddle. If he did not know the answer, he lost his life.

"So for her many a poor creature did die, as yonder grim looks do testify."

Gower pointed to some decapitated heads that had been stuck on the ends of spikes.

He continued, "What now follows in this book, I give to the judgment of your eyes. You will be the judges of what follows and decide if it is good or bad. You will judge for yourself whether this book gladdens your spirits."

In a garden of King Antiochus' palace in Antioch, Antiochus and Pericles, Prince of Tyre, talked. Pericles had come to Antiochus' palace in order to make Antiochus' daughter his wife.

King Antiochus said, "Young Prince of Tyre, you have fully heard about the danger of the task you undertake."

"I have, Antiochus, and with a soul emboldened with the glory of your daughter's praise, I think that death is no hazard in this enterprise."

"Bring in our daughter, clothed like a bride for the embraces even of Jupiter, King of the gods, himself," King Antiochus said. "From my daughter's conception until Lucina, goddess of childbirth, reigned, Nature gave my daughter this dowry: To gladden my daughter, the senate-house of planets all did sit and gave her their best perfections. All the astrological signs were propitious from the time my daughter was conceived until she was born."

Music played, and King Antiochus' daughter entered the garden.

"See where she comes, clothed like the Spring," Pericles said. "The Three Graces — sister goddesses who bestow beauty and charm — are her subjects, and her thoughts dwell on the Kingliest form of every virtue that gives renown to men! Her face is the book of memorable praises, where is read nothing but exquisite pleasures, as if from thence sorrow had been forever erased and testy wrath could never be her mild companion.

"You gods who made me man, and made me sway in love, who have inflamed desire in my breast to taste the fruit, the daughter, of yonder celestial tree, Antiochus, or die in the attempt, be my helpers, as I am son and servant to your will — help me to achieve such a boundless happiness!"

"Prince Pericles —" Antiochus began.

Pericles interrupted, "— who would be a son-in-law to great Antiochus."

Antiochus continued, "Before you stands this fair garden of the Hesperides, with golden fruit, but dangerous to be touched, for deadly dragons are here to fiercely frighten you."

One of Hercules' twelve labors was to go to the garden of the Hesperides — goddesses of the evening — and steal some golden apples that were guarded by a hundred-headed dragon.

Antiochus continued, "My daughter's face, like Heaven, entices you to view her countless — as numerous as the stars — glories, which merit must gain. If you lack the merit to achieve my daughter, then because your eye presumes to acquire what it does not deserve, all the entire heap of your body must die."

Antiochus pointed to the decapitated heads and said, "These once famous Princes, like yourself, drawn by reports of my daughter's graces, made adventurous by desire for her, tell you, with the speechless tongues and pale faces, that without any covering, save a field of stars, here they stand martyrs, slain in Cupid's wars, and with their dead cheeks they advise you to desist from going so early into the net of Death, whom none can resist."

"Antiochus, I thank you," Pericles said. "You have taught me to know that I am frail and mortal, and you have used those fearful objects — those heads impaled on spikes — to prepare this body, which is similar to their bodies, for what I must do someday, which is to die.

"For death remembered should be like a mirror, which tells us that life is only breath, and to trust that we will continue always to live is an error. For mortal men, death is not optional."

Mirrors are used to see if someone is dead. The mirror is held against the person's nose and mouth. If the person is breathing, mist appears on the mirror.

Pericles continued, "I'll make my will then, and I will do as sick men do who know the world and see Heaven, but, feeling woe, they do not grasp at Earthly joys as formerly they did. Heaven is preferable to ill life on Earth.

"So in my will I bequeath a happy peace to you and to all good men, as every Prince should do. If I die, do not feel guilty."

Pericles then looked at Antiochus' daughter and said, "My riches — my body — will return to the Earth from whence they came, but I leave my unspotted and pure fire of love to you."

He continued, "Thus ready for the way of life or the way of death, I await the sharpest blow, Antiochus."

"Since you scorn and reject advice," Antiochus replied, "read the riddle out loud. If you cannot solve the riddle after you have read it, it is decreed that like these Princes who tried and failed before you, you yourself shall bleed."

Antiochus' daughter said, "In all save this, may you prove to be successful! In all save this, I wish you happiness!"

She did not want her sin — committing incest with her father — to be made known, so she did not want Pericles to solve the riddle; however, Pericles had made enough of an impression on her that she did not want him to die.

Pericles said, "Like a bold champion, I enter the combat arena, and I do not ask help from any other thought except faithfulness and courage."

He read the riddle out loud:

"I am no viper, yet I feed
"On mother's flesh which did me breed."

The first two lines referred to the belief that vipers were born by eating their way out of their mother's body.

"I sought a husband, in which labor
"I found that kindness in a father:
"He's father, son, and husband mild;
"I mother, wife, and yet his child.
"How they may be, and yet in two,
"As you will live, resolve it you."

Pericles solved the riddle immediately, but solving it gave him no pleasure: King Antiochus and his daughter were incestuous lovers.

Of course, the daughter was the child of King Antiochus. Because she was sleeping with him, it was as if she were his wife. Because she was sleeping with him, it was if she had taken the place of her mother.

Of course, King Antiochus was the father of his daughter. Because he was sleeping with her, it was as if he were her husband. Because he was sleeping with his daughter and because it was as if she had taken the place of her mother, it was as if he were her son-in-law.

Pericles thought, *The last line of the riddle is strong medicine. If I want to live, I must solve the riddle, and I must show that I have solved it by stating the answer out loud. Since King Antiochus will hardly want his sin to be publicly known, I will be killed whether I speak up or not. You powers who give Heaven countless eyes — stars — to view men's acts, why haven't you clouded those eyes perpetually and kept this sin hidden if this sin is true — this sin which makes me pale to read it?*

Pericles looked at Antiochus' daughter and said to her, "Fair glass of light, I loved you, and could still, were not this glorious casket stored with ill."

The daughter was like a looking glass, a mirror. It reflected but did not contain light. Its appearance was beautiful, but its reality was not beautiful. The daughter's body was like a beautiful casket, but what was inside — her soul — was ill.

Pericles continued, "But I must tell you, now my thoughts revolt — he's no man on whom perfections wait who, knowing sin is within, will touch the gate."

In this society, "gate" was slang for "vagina."

Pericles continued, "You are a fair viol, and your body and senses are the strings. If your strings were fingered to make lawful music for a man, as a husband and a wife can lawfully do, then Heaven and all the gods would come down to Earth to listen.

"But your strings have been played upon before the right time. Only Hell dances to so harsh a music.

"Truly, I do not care for you."

Pericles made a movement that King Antiochus interpreted as Pericles' being about to touch his daughter, and he immediately warned him, "Prince Pericles, do not touch my daughter, upon your life. If you touch her, you die. That's an article within our law — this article is as dangerous as anything else in our law. Your time is up. Either give the answer to the riddle now, or receive your sentence."

"Great King," Pericles said, "few love to hear the sins they love to act; it would touch yourself too nearly for me to tell the answer to the riddle. Whoever has a book of all the actions that monarchs do will be safer if he keeps that book shut than if he shows it to others.

"Vice gossiped about is like the wandering wind. As the gossip spreads his news, he blows dust in others' eyes. Sometimes the gossip deceives others, and sometimes the news is true. The gossip's news irritates both the hearers and the guilty parties. This is done at a high price. After the gossip has spread the news, the sore eyes of the guilty see clearly who is spreading the news, and to stop the news being spread further, they hurt the gossip.

"The blind mole casts peaked hills — molehills — towards Heaven, to reveal that the Earth is crushed by man's sins; and the poor mole dies for it."

A mole builds molehills like men of excessive pride built the tower of Babel to reach Heaven, and so each molehill is a reminder of men's sin. By building the molehill and broadcasting news of men's sins, the mole reveals its presence and the gardener kills it.

Pericles continued, "Kings are the gods of Earth; when it comes to vice, their law is their will — they do whatever they want. If Jupiter should stray and commit adultery, as he has many, many times, who dares to say that Jupiter commits a sin?

"It is enough that you know that I know, and it is fitting to smother news of a sin when the sin grows worse when it is widely known.

"All love the womb that first gave birth to their being, so then give my tongue similar permission to love my head."

Pericles was telling King Antiochus that he preferred being silent to losing his head. He was willing to keep King Antiochus' secret if the King would allow him to live. Earlier, the King's daughter had made it clear that she did not want her secret sin to be revealed and that she did not want Pericles to die, so her wishes might make her father more merciful to Pericles.

King Antiochus thought, *By Heaven, I wish that I had your head! I would like to have your intelligence. I also would like to have your head off your shoulders so that I can be certain that my secret is not publicly revealed. Pericles has found the meaning of the riddle, but I will speak duplicitous flattering words to him.*

He said, "Young Prince of Tyre, though by the terms of our strict law, because you have not explained the riddle, we might proceed to cancel all of your days and have you killed immediately, yet hope, proceeding from so fair a tree as your fair self — we hope that you will have fruit, aka children, one day — does importune us to do otherwise. We will give you a respite of forty more days, if by which time you reveal the secret of the riddle, this mercy shows that we will take joy in such a son-in-law. Until then your entertainment here shall be as befits our honor and your merit."

Everyone left except Pericles, who said to himself, "King Antiochus' courtesy is an attempt to cover up his sin, but this is done by a hypocrite who is good in nothing except appearance! If it were true that I solved the riddle incorrectly, then it would be certain that you — Antiochus — were not so bad as with foul incest to abuse your soul. However, you're both a father and a son-in-law because of your ill and untimely claspings with your child. That kind of pleasure is fitting for a husband, not a father, and she has become an eater of her mother's flesh because of her defiling of her parents' bed. She has taken her mother's place in her father's bed, and she has taken the pleasure reserved for the mother. Both are like serpents, for although father and daughter feed on sweetest flowers, yet they breed poison.

"Antioch, farewell! Wisdom knows that those men who do not blush as they perform actions blacker than the night will shun no course of action to keep those black actions from the light.

"One sin, I know, another does provoke; murder is as near to lust as flame is to smoke. Poison and treason are the hands of sin, yes, and also the shields to ward off the shame.

"So then, lest my life be cut down to keep you, King Antiochus, clear, with my flight I'll shun the danger that I fear."

Pericles left the garden, and King Antiochus returned to it.

King Antiochus said to himself, "Pericles has found the meaning of the riddle, for which we mean to have his decapitated head. He must not live to trumpet forth my infamy, nor tell the world that I, Antiochus, sin in such a loathed manner, and therefore immediately this Prince must die, for by his fall my honor must remain high."

He said loudly, "Who is waiting on us?"

Thaliard, an important lord, entered the garden and asked, "Is your Highness calling me?"

Using the royal plural, King Antiochus replied, "You are of our inner circle, and you know our secrets. Because of your faithfulness to us, we will advance and promote you."

He gave Thaliard some items and said, "Thaliard, look, here's poison, and here's gold. We hate Pericles, the Prince of Tyre, and you must kill him. Don't ask the reason why. It is enough that you know we want you to kill him. Tell me, will it be done?"

"My lord, it will be done."

"Good."

A messenger, out of breath because he had hurried to bring King Antiochus important news, ran into the garden.

King Antiochus said to him, "Let your breathing cool yourself as you tell us the reason for your haste."

The messenger said, "My lord, Prince Pericles has fled," and then he left.

King Antiochus said to Thaliard, "If you want to continue to live, run after Pericles, and like an arrow shot by a much-experienced archer hits the target that his eyes aim at, make sure that you never return here unless you can tell me, 'Prince Pericles is dead.'"

Thaliard replied, "My lord, if I can get him within the range of my pistol, I'll kill him — he will be sure to do no damage to you. So, farewell to your Highness."

"Thaliard, *adieu*!"

Thaliard exited.

King Antiochus said to himself, "Until Pericles is dead, my heart can lend no relief to my head."

Pericles had returned to Tyre and was standing in a room of his palace.

Pericles said to the lords who were just outside the room, "Let no one disturb us."

He then said to himself, "Why should this change of thoughts, this sad companion, this dull-eyed melancholy, be my so accustomed guest that not an hour, whether in the Sun's glorious walk across the sky, or in the peaceful night, which is the tomb where grief should sleep, can produce for me quiet? I used to be happy, but now I am continually melancholy.

"Here pleasures court my eyes, but my eyes shun them, and danger, which I feared, is at Antioch, the aim of whose King seems far too short to hit me here. Yet neither pleasure's art can add joy to my spirits, nor can danger's distance comfort me.

"Then this must be true: The passionate feelings of the mind, which have their first conception by misdread — the fear of evil — have later sustenance and life by worry. And what was at first only fear of what might happen, grows elder now and takes action so that what is feared does not happen.

"And so it is with me. The great Antiochus, against whom I am too little to contend, since he's so great that he can do whatever he wants, will think I am speaking to others about his sin, although I swear that I am silent. Nor will it help me if I say that I honor him if he suspects that I may dishonor him by revealing his sin. Knowing that it would make him blush if it were known, he'll stop the course by which it might be known. To keep me from talking about his sin, he will kill me.

"With hostile forces he'll overspread our land, and with the show of war he will look so huge that terror shall drive courage from our state. Our men will be vanquished before they resist, and our subjects will be punished although they have never thought of causing offense.

"My concern for them, not pity for myself, who am no more but as the tops of trees, which guard the roots they grow by and defend them, makes both my body pine and my soul languish, and it punishes me before Antiochus can punish me."

Helicanus, who was an older lord, and some other lords entered the room.

The first lord said to Pericles, "May joy and all comfort be in your sacred breast!"

The second lord said, "May joy and all comfort, until you return to us, keep you peaceful and comfortable!"

The lords were aware that Pericles had been melancholy lately. They were wishing peaceful and comfortable feelings for Pericles until he returned to normal and became a man of action again.

Helicanus, however, objected to this. Instead of the lords' encouraging Pericles to be inactive, he felt that they should encourage him to immediately cast off his melancholy and immediately become a man of action again.

"Peace, peace, and let an experienced man speak," Helicanus said. "They who flatter the King abuse him, for flattery is the bellows that blows up sin. The thing that is flattered is only a spark, to which the blast of the bellows gives heat and stronger glowing. Flattery misleads Kings and encourages them to do the wrong thing.

"In contrast, reproof, when obedient and in order, befits Kings, as they are men, for men and Kings may err."

Referring to the second lord, Helicanus said, "When Signior Flattery here advises peace for you, he flatters you: He tells you that your inactivity is justified, and in so doing he makes war upon your life."

Seeing that Pericles looked angry, Helicanus knelt and said, "Prince, pardon me, or strike me, if you please. I cannot be much lower than my knees."

Pericles said to the other lords, "All except Helicanus leave us, but take care to go to the harbor and see what ships and cargoes are there. I must be on the lookout for ships from Antioch. Once you are done, return to us."

This may have gladdened Helicanus — Pericles was taking at least a little action. However, Pericles was angry at Helicanus' criticism of the second lord — and Pericles wanted to wallow in his melancholy.

The lords exited, and using the royal plural, Pericles said, "Helicanus, you have moved us emotionally. What emotion do you see in our face?"

"I see an angry brow, deeply honored lord."

"If there is such an arrow in the frowns of Princes, how can your tongue dare to make me angry and show anger in our face?"

"How dare the plants look up to Heaven, from whence they receive their nourishment?"

"You know that I have the power to take your life from you," Pericles said.

"I have sharpened the axe myself; all you have to do is strike the blow."

Pericles stopped being angry; Helicanus was a good and loyal lord.

"Rise, please, rise," Pericles said. "Sit down. You are no flatterer. I thank you for it, and Heaven forbid that Kings should let their ears hear words that hide the Kings' faults! You are a fitting counselor and servant for a Prince, who by your wisdom make a Prince your servant — a wise Prince will follow wise advice. What do you want me to do?"

"I want you to bear with patience such griefs as you yourself lay upon yourself. I want you to stop moping about and become again a man of action."

Pericles replied, "You speak like a physician, Helicanus, who gives a potion to me that you would tremble to take yourself.

"Listen to me, therefore, and let me give you more information about what has happened to me. I went to Antioch, where as you know, against the face of death, I sought the acquisition of a glorious beauty with whom I might have children — children who are a strength to Princes and a joy to the Prince's subjects. Her face was to my eye beyond all wonder. The rest — listen carefully — was as black as incest. After the sinful father realized that I knew that he had committed incest, he put on an appearance. Instead of striking me, he flattered me with smooth words. But as you know, it is time to fear when tyrants seem to kiss.

"Such fear so grew in me, I fled back home, here, under the protective covering of night, which seemed to be my good guardian, and, once I was here, I thought about what was past, and what the future might bring.

"I knew that Antiochus was tyrannous, and we know that tyrants' fears do not decrease — instead, they grow faster than the years. And should he fear, as no doubt he does, that I should reveal to the listening air how many worthy Princes had their blood shed to keep his incestuous bed of blackness secret, then to stop that fear he'll fill this land with weapons and soldiers, and pretend that I have done something wrong to him.

"I realize that everyone in this land, including the innocent, must feel war's blow because of my offense — if I can call it offense. I love all of my subjects, of which you yourself are one, and you just now criticized me for my melancholy —"

"Alas, sir!"

"I know that a tempest is coming to this land. I have drawn sleep out of my eyes and blood from my cheeks, and I have placed musings into my mind, along with a thousand fears, as I tried to find a way for me to stop this tempest before it came, but I found little that would comfort and relieve my mind. I thought it Princely charity to grieve for my subjects. This is why I have been melancholy."

"Well, my lord, since you have given me leave to speak, I will speak freely," Helicanus said. "You regard me as a wise and loyal counselor, and I will try to give you wise and loyal advice. You fear Antiochus, and justly, too, I think. You fear the tyrant, who either by public war or by private treason will take away your life and kill you.

"Therefore, my lord, I advise you to go and travel for a while, until Antiochus' rage and anger are forgotten, or until the Destinies — the Fates — cut his thread of life.

"Delegate your authority to rule to anyone you choose; if you delegate it to me, day will not serve light more faithfully than I'll serve you."

"I do not doubt your loyalty," Pericles said, "but what if he should wrong my liberties — my royal prerogatives, my territories, my subjects' freedoms — in my absence?"

Helicanus' advice was good. If Pericles were not at Tyre, Antiochus' making war against Tyre would not result in Pericles' death. Therefore, Antiochus was much less likely to attack Tyre if Pericles was no longer there. Still, Pericles was cautious. He wanted his subjects to be safe.

Helicanus knew that sometimes force had to be met with force, although it is better to use diplomacy and seek peace.

He replied, "If that should happen, we'll mingle our bloods together in the earth, from whence we had our being and our birth."

Pericles became a man of action again.

He said, "I now look away from you, Tyre, and I intend to travel to Tarsus, where I'll hear from you, Helicanus, and I'll act in accordance with the information I read in your letters to me. The care I had and have to ensure my subjects' good I lay on you whose wisdom's strength can bear it. I have acted to take good care of my subjects, and in my absence I give you my authority, which I expect you to use to take good care of my subjects. I'll take your word that you will do this, and I will not ask you to take an oath. Anyone who will break his word will also break his oath. But in our separate spheres of action, we'll live so honestly and trustworthily that time shall never confute this truth of both of us: You are a loyal subject, and I am a true Prince."

15

Thaliard had arrived in Tyre on his mission to assassinate Pericles, its Prince.

Standing in an antechamber of the palace, he said to himself, "So, this is Tyre, and this is the court. Here I must kill King Pericles, and if I do not kill him, I am sure to be hanged at home. This job is dangerous.

"Well, I perceive that the ancient poet Philippides was a wise fellow, and had good discretion, in that, when he was told to ask for what he wanted from the King, he desired that he might know none of his secrets. Now I see he had some reason for it, for if a King orders a man to be a villain, that man is bound by the contract of his oath to be a villain!

"Quiet! Here come the lords of Tyre."

Helicanus and Escanes, and other lords of Tyre, entered the antechamber. Helicanus immediately recognized Thaliard, who was an important lord of Antioch, but pretended not to see him. The information that he was going to now give to the lords, he knew would be overheard by Thaliard.

Helicanus said, "You shall not need, my fellow peers of Tyre, to question me further about your King's departure. His commission, which bears the royal seal and gives me authority to act for him, he left in trust with me. It communicates sufficiently that he's gone to travel."

Thaliard thought, *What! King Pericles is gone!*

Helicanus continued, "If you want further information about why, without your loving permission, he would leave Tyre, I can give some light to you. While he was at Antioch ..."

Thaliard thought, *What about his being at Antioch?*

Helicanus continued, "... royal Antiochus — for what reason I don't know — took some displeasure at him; at least Prince Pericles judged this to be the case. And fearing lest that he had erred or sinned, to show his sorrow, he decided to reprimand himself, and so he put himself to the toil of a sailor, to whom each minute can bring life or death. Pericles is now traveling on the seas."

Thaliard thought, *Well, I see that I shall not be hanged now, although I would be if Pericles were here and I did not kill him. But since Pericles has gone, the King's ears will be pleased to hear that Pericles has escaped death on the land, only to perish at sea. I will tell King Antiochus that Pericles drowned at sea. But now I'll present myself to Helicanus.*

He said loudly, "Peace to the lords of Tyre!"

Helicanus was a good advisor and a good leader. He wished the peace between Antioch and Tyre to continue, and so he intended to treat Thaliard well.

He said, "Lord Thaliard from Antiochus is welcome."

Thaliard replied, "From him I have come with a message for Princely Pericles, but since my landing I have understood that your lord has taken himself to unknown travels, and so my message must return to where it came from."

"We have no reason to desire to see the message," Helicanus replied, "since it is addressed to our master, not to us. Yet, before you depart, we desire, since we are friends to Antioch, that we and you may feast in Tyre."

— 1.4 —

Cleon, the governor of Tarsus, and his wife, Dionyza, were outside the governor's house in Tarsus. Around them were other people, including starving citizens of Tarsus.

Cleon said, "My Dionyza, shall we rest ourselves here, and by relating tales of the griefs of other people, see if it will help us to forget our own?"

"To do so would be like blowing on a fire in hopes to put it out," Dionyza replied. "Whoever digs on a hill to lower it because it rises high accomplishes nothing except to move dirt from one spot to another. He throws down one mountain only to cast up a higher. My distressed lord, our griefs are like that. Here we feel them, and we look around and see them with our eyes because they afflict other people, but our griefs are similar to groves; after they are pruned, they rise higher. If we were to try to forget our griefs by talking about the griefs of other people, it would only make us feel our griefs more sharply."

"Oh, Dionyza, who lacks food, and will not say he wants it? Who can conceal his hunger until he starves? Our sorrowful tongues deeply sound our woes into the air; our eyes weep while our lungs draw in breath so that our tongues may proclaim our griefs louder so that, if the gods slumber while their creatures lack food, our tongues may awaken the gods so that the gods may comfort their creatures. I will now talk about our woes, which we have felt for several years. When I lack breath to speak, help me with your tears."

"I'll do my best, sir," Dionyza replied.

"This is Tarsus," Cleon said, "over which I govern. It is a city over which Copia, the goddess of abundance and plenty, held out a full hand, for she strewed riches even in the streets. Our city's towers bore tops so high they kissed the clouds, and strangers never beheld our city without admiring it. Our city's men and dames so strutted and adorned themselves that each was like a mirror for another person to use while dressing. Their tables were heaped full of food, to gladden the sight, and the purpose of the food was not so much to feed on as to delight. All poverty was scorned, and pride was so great that people hated to use the word 'help.'"

"That is so true," Dionyza said.

"But see what Heaven can do!" Cleon said. "Just recently, the earth, sea, and air, although they gave their creatures in abundance, were all too little to content and please the mouths of our citizens. But things have changed, and these mouths are like houses that become dirty and polluted because they are not used — these mouths are now starved for want of exercise. They have nothing to chew and eat. Those palates that, not even two summers ago, required fresh, novel dishes to delight the taste, would now be glad to taste bread, and they beg for it. Those mothers who, to rear and bring up their babes, thought nothing too finely and elaborately made, are so hungry that they are ready now to eat those little darlings whom they loved. So sharp are hunger's teeth that man and wife draw lots to see who first shall die to lengthen the other's life. With one dead, the other has more food, and the living may feast on the dead. Here stands a lord and there stands a lady weeping. Here many sink dead to the ground, yet those who see them fall have scarcely enough strength left to give them burial. Isn't this true?"

"Our hollow cheeks and hollow eyes are evidence that it is true," Dionyza said.

"Oh, let those cities that of the goddess of plenty's cup and her prosperities so largely taste with their wasteful, indulgent behavior hear this weeping and see these tears! The misery of Tarsus may be theirs."

A lord arrived and asked, "Where's the lord governor?"

"Here," Cleon said. "Speak out your sorrows that you bring in haste, for comfort is too much for us to expect. We no longer expect to hear good news — only bad."

"We have sighted, upon our neighboring shore, stately sails of ships coming here."

"This is bad news," Cleon said. "I thought as much. One sorrow never comes but it brings an heir that may follow as its inheritor. And so it happens with our sorrow. We are weak from famine, and so some neighboring nation, taking advantage of our misery, has stuffed these hollow vessels with their soldiers to beat us down, although we are down already. They want to make a conquest of unhappy me, although there is no glory in overcoming someone as weak as me."

"We need not worry about that," the lord said, "for, by the appearance of the white flags the ships are displaying, they bring us peace and have come to us as helpers, not as foes."

"You speak like a person who has not been taught to recite this proverb: Who makes the fairest show means the most deceit. But bring they what they will and what they can, what need we fear? The ground's the lowest we can fall, and we are halfway there. We are on our knees and stooped over. Go tell their general we await him here to find out why he comes, from where he comes, and what he wants."

"I go to do my duty, my lord."

The lord exited.

"Welcome is peace, if their general on peace insists. If he insists on war, we are unable to resist," Cleon said.

Pericles arrived with some attendants and said to Cleon, "Lord governor, for so we hear you are, let not our ships and the number of our men be like a beacon set on fire to terrify your eyes."

People of the time guarded the coast. If they saw enemy ships arriving, they lit beacon fires to alert others that an invasion was coming.

Pericles continued, "We have heard about your miseries as far away as Tyre, and we have seen the desolation of your streets. We do not come to add sorrow to your tears, but to relieve them of the heavy sorrows that cause them. These our hollow ships, which you perhaps may think are like the hollow Trojan Horse that was stuffed with bloodthirsty soldiers waiting to come out and overthrow the city, are instead stored with grain to make your necessary bread, and give life to them whom hunger has starved half dead."

Cleon, Dionyza, and the starving citizens of Tarsus who were present knelt and said, "May the gods of Greece protect you! And we'll pray for you."

"Arise, please, arise," Pericles said. Using the royal plural, he added, "We do not look for reverence, but for friendship and harborage for ourself, our ships, and our men."

Cleon replied, "You will have both friendship and harborage here. When anyone in Tarsus shall not give you those things, or if they repay you with unthankfulness in thought, whether it be our wives, our children, or ourselves, then may the curse of Heaven and men follow their evils! Until that time — which I hope never shall come — your grace is welcome to our town and us."

"We accept your welcome," Pericles said, "and we will feast here awhile, until our stars that now frown lend us a smile."

CHAPTER 2

— Prologue —

Addressing you the reader, John Gower said, "Here you have seen a mighty King, Antiochus, indeed, his child to incest bring. You have also seen a better Prince and benign lord — Pericles — who will prove to be worthy of awe both in deed and word. He will be quiet and patient, as men should be, until he has endured adversity.

"I'll show you that those who among troubles reign, by losing a mite, a mountain gain. Pericles, who is good in conduct and to whom I give my blessing, is still at Tarsus, where each citizen thinks that everything he speaks is holy writ, and to commemorate what he does and has done, they build a statue of him to make him glorious. But tidings to the contrary — bad tidings — are now brought before your eyes, so what need do I have to speak?"

A dumb show — a show without speaking — appears in your brain, and you see Pericles and Cleon walk through one door with all their train of attendants following them. A gentleman bearing a letter walks through another door and gives the letter to Pericles, who reads it and then shows it to Cleon. Pericles then gives the messenger a monetary reward and knights him. Pericles exits through one door, and Cleon exits through another door.

John Gower said, "Good Helicanus stayed at home, not to eat honey — the result of the labor of others — like a drone, but instead to strive to kill bad and to keep good alive as well as to fulfill his Prince's desires. Good Helicanus always sends word to Pericles of all that happens in Tyre. In this letter, he told Pericles about how Thaliard came fully determined to sin and had the intention of murdering him. Helicanus also advised Pericles that he ought not to stay longer in Tarsus — it was not best for him there to make his rest.

"Pericles, taking Helicanus' advice, sailed on the seas, where when men are, there is seldom ease. Now the wind begins to blow, and with thunder above and deeps below, the winds create such unquiet that the ship that should keep Pericles safe is wrecked and split, and he, good Prince, having lost everything, by waves from coast to coast is tossed. All the men perish, all possessions are lost, and no one and nothing escapes except himself. Finally, Lady Fortune, tired with doing bad, threw Pericles ashore, to make him glad.

"Look, here he comes. What shall be next, pardon old Gower, for he shall not tell you — what shall be next belongs to the text."

Pericles, dripping wet, stood on a seashore of Pentapolis, whose King was Simonides. The day was still stormy, although the storm was lessening.

Pericles addressed the stars: "Now cease your ire, you angry stars of Heaven! Wind, rain, and thunder, remember that Earthly man is just a substance that must yield to you, and I, as befits my Earthly nature, obey you.

"Unfortunately, the sea has cast me on the rocks, washed me from shore to shore, and left me breath — life — with nothing to think about except my ensuing death.

"Let it suffice the greatness of your powers to have bereft a Prince of all his fortunes, and having thrown him from your watery grave, here to have death in peace is all he'll crave."

Three fishermen were on the shore, but they did not notice Pericles. Because of the loudness of the lessening storm, they talked loudly.

The third fisherman was deep in thought. The first and second fishermen were ready to get to work.

The first fisherman called to the third fisherman, "What, ho, Pilch!"

A pilch is a leather jacket.

The second fisherman called, "Ha, come and bring away the nets!"

The fisherman called, "What, Patchbreech, I say!"

In addition to wearing a leather jacket, the third fisherman wore patched trousers.

"What do you want, master?" the third fisherman asked.

"Look at how you are waking up now! Get busy and start working, or I'll fetch you with a vengeance. I'll beat you to wake you so that you can work."

"Truly, master, I am thinking of the poor men who were cast into the sea and drowned in front of us just now," the third fishermen said to explain his pensiveness.

"Oh, those poor souls," the first fisherman said. "It grieved my heart to hear what pitiful cries they made to us to help them, when, sadly, we could scarcely even help ourselves."

"Master, didn't I say as much when I saw the porpoise bounce and plunge in the sea — a sure sign of a storm?" the third fisherman said. "People say porpoises are half fish and half flesh — a plague on them. Every time I see them, I expect to be washed into the sea. Master, I wonder how the fishes live in the sea."

"Why, they live in the sea just like men do on land," the first fisherman said. "The great ones eat up the little ones. I can compare our rich misers to nothing as suitably as to a whale. The whale plays and plunges, driving the poor fry — the small fish — before him, and at last devours them all at a mouthful. I have heard that such whales are living on the land; they never close their mouths until after they've swallowed the whole parish — church, steeple, bells, and all."

Pericles said softly to himself, "A pretty moral."

The third fisherman said, "But, master, if I had been the sexton, and in charge of the bells, I would have been that day in the belfry."

"Why, man?" the second fisherman asked.

"So that the whale would have swallowed me, too," the third fisherman said. "When I would be in his belly, I would have kept such a jangling of the bells that he would never have left until he vomited bells, steeple, church, and parish up again. But if the good King Simonides were of my mind —"

Pericles said softly to himself, "Simonides."

The third fisherman continued, "— we would purge the land of these lazy drones who rob the bee of her honey."

Pericles said softly to himself, "These fishermen tell about the infirmities of men, using what they have learned from the finny subjects of the sea. From the fishes' watery empire, these fishermen gather up all that men may approve or men may detect to be evil!"

Deciding to reveal himself to the three fishermen, Pericles said loudly, "Peace be at your labor, honest fishermen."

The second fisherman said to Pericles, who looked bedraggled and as if he might be a beggar, "Honest and good fellow, what's that? Peaceful labor! On a stormy day like this! If you think this is a good day, take it out of the calendar and examine it closely. Nobody will go looking for it!"

Pericles said, "You may see that the sea has cast upon your coast —"

The second fisherman interrupted, "What a drunken knave was the sea to cast you in our way!"

Pericles continued, "— a man whom both the waters and the wind, in that vast tennis court, have made the ball for them to play with, a man who entreats you to pity him. This he asks of you although he is a man who never used to beg."

"No, friend, cannot you beg?" the first fisherman said. "Some people in our country — Greece — get more with begging than we do with working."

"Can you catch any fishes, then?" the second fisherman said.

"I have never done the work of a fisherman," Pericles replied.

"Then you will surely starve," the second fisherman said, "for there's nothing to be got here nowadays, unless you can fish for it."

"What I have been, I have forgotten," Pericles said.

Of course, Pericles had lived like the Prince he was, but now he was needy.

He continued, "But what I am, need teaches me to think on — I am a man burdened by cold. My veins are chilled, and they have no more of life than may suffice to give my tongue enough heat to ask for your help. If you should refuse to help me, then when I am dead, please see that I am buried because I am a man."

"When he is dead, he says?" the first fisherman said. "Gods forbid! I have a sea-coat here. Come, put it on; it will keep you warm. Now, I say, here is a handsome fellow! Come, you shall go home and stay with me, and we'll have flesh for holidays, fish for fasting days, and also we'll have sausages and pancakes, and you shall be welcome."

"I thank you, sir," Pericles said.

"Listen, my friend," the second fisherman said. "You said you could not beg."

Pericles replied, "I did not beg, but I did crave."

This was a bit of a joke because begging and craving are much the same thing.

"Crave!" the second fisherman said. "Then I'll turn craver, too, and so I shall escape whipping."

"Why, are all your beggars whipped, then?" Pericles asked.

In this society, the beadle punished able-bodied beggars by whipping them.

"Oh, not all, my friend," the second fisherman replied, "not all; for if all your beggars were whipped, I would wish no better job than to be beadle."

He then said to the first fisherman, "But, master, I'll go draw up the net."

The second and the third fishermen exited.

Pericles thought, *How well this honest mirth becomes their labor!*

The first fisherman asked him, "Sir, do you know where you are?"

"Not well."

"Why, then I'll tell you," the first fisherman said. "This place is called Pentapolis, and our King is the good Simonides."

"The good King Simonides, do you call him?" Pericles asked.

"Yes, sir, and he deserves to be called good because of his peaceful reign and good government."

"He is a happy King, since he gains from his subjects the name of good for his government," Pericles said. "How far is his court from this shore?"

"Sir, half a day's journey, and I'll tell you that he has a fair daughter, and tomorrow is her birthday; and Princes and knights have come from all parts of the world to joust in a tournament for her love."

"If my fortunes were equal to my desires, I could wish to make one there," Pericles said.

"Oh, sir, things must be as they may," the first fisherman said, "and what a man cannot get, he may lawfully deal for his wife's soul."

No man can beget a child by himself alone, but he can beget a child — lawfully — by marrying a woman and becoming one with her. That is the way that things are.

If Pericles is to have his fortunes equal to his desires, he will need help from others. He cannot do it alone. That is the way that things are.

The second and the third fishermen came back, dragging their net.

The second fisherman said, "Help, master, help! Here's a fish caught in the net, like a poor man who is in the right, according to the law; it will hardly come out."

This was a cynical joke. A poor man, although he is in the right, may be trapped in the legal system and find it difficult to escape, just like a poor fish caught in a net. Still, the joke did not say that it was impossible to escape.

The second fisherman pulled the "fish" out of the net and said, "Ha! The plague on it! The 'fish' has come out at last, and it has turned into rusty armor."

"Armor, my friends!" Pericles said. "Please, let me see it."

He recognized it as his father's armor, which had been on board the ship that wrecked, and he prayed, "Thanks, Lady Fortune, who, after all my crosses, have given me something with which to repair myself."

Pericles intended to repair his fortunes by fighting in and winning the tournament.

Pericles continued his prayer to Lady Fortune, "You gave this armor to me although it is my own, part of my heritage, which my dead father bequeathed to me. He gave me this strict charge, even as he left his life, 'Keep it, my Pericles; it has been a shield between me and death. Because it saved me, keep it; in like necessity — which I pray the gods will protect you from! — this armor may protect you.'"

He said to the fishermen, "Wherever I have gone, I have taken this armor — I kept it where I kept myself because I so dearly loved it — until the rough seas, which spare no man, took it away from me in rage, although the seas, now calmed, have given it to me again.

"I thank you for it: my shipwreck is now not so ill since I have here a gift that my father gave me in his will."

"What do you mean, sir?" the first fisherman asked.

"I mean to beg of you, kind friends, this coat of worth," Pericles said. "For it was once the protector of a King. I know it by this mark."

Of course, the armor had been used in battle. Pericles pointed to a mark that an enemy's weapon had made.

He added, "The King loved me dearly, and for his sake I wish the having of his armor. And I wish that you will guide me to your sovereign's court, where with this armor I may appear as a gentleman. If my low fortune ever becomes better, I'll repay you for your good deeds; until then I will be your debtor."

"Do you intend to compete in the tournament for the lady, the King's daughter?" the first fisherman asked.

"I intend to show the skill that I have in arms," Pericles said.

"Take the armor, and may the gods give you good fortune to go with it!" said the first fisherman, who began to help Pericles put on the armor.

"Yes, but listen, my friend; it was we who made up this garment through the rough seams of the waters," the second fisherman said.

He was punning by using words appropriate to tailoring. One job of tailors is to make up a suit that has seams.

The second fisherman added, "There are certain condolements, certain vails."

The second fisherman wanted a reward for finding the armor. "Condolements" was a malapropism for "doles," aka gifts. "Vails" were tips; the word also referred to the scrap material left over after a tailor finished making a garment — the tailor kept the scrap material.

"I hope, sir," the second fisherman added, "that if you thrive, you'll remember where you got this armor."

"Believe it, I will," Pericles said. He was now wearing the armor, and he looked much more like a gentleman.

He added, "By your assistance, I am clothed in steel, and, despite all the violence of the sea that has violently seized almost everything that was onboard the ship that wrecked, a jeweled bracelet still keeps its place on my arm."

Pericles said to the jeweled bracelet, "I will use all your value to acquire a courser that I will mount and ride in the tournament. My horse's delightful steps shall make the gazer rejoice to see him tread."

Pericles then said to the second fisherman, "Only, my friend, I still lack a pair of bases — a divided skirt that knights wear over their armor while on horseback."

"We'll surely provide it," the second fisherman said. "You shall have my best sea-coat to make yourself a pair of bases, and I'll bring you to the court myself."

Pericles replied, "Then let honor be a goal for my will; this day I'll rise, or else add ill to ill."

King Simonides and his daughter, Thaisa, stood by the lists — the ground where the tournament would take place. With them were lords and attendants.

King Simonides asked a lord, "Are the knights ready to begin the tournament?"

The lord replied, "They are, my liege, and they await your coming to present themselves to you and your daughter."

"Take this answer to them: We are ready; and our daughter, in honor of whose birth this tournament is being held, sits here, like beauty's child, whom nature gave birth to for men to see and wonder at."

The lord exited, and Thaisa said, "It pleases you, my royal father, to praise me much more than I deserve."

"It's fitting it should be so," King Simonides replied, "for Princesses are a model that Heaven makes similar to itself. As jewelry loses its glory if neglected, so Princesses lose their renown if not valued and respected."

He added, "It is now your honorable duty, daughter, to view the purpose of each knight as expressed in his device."

The device was a small shield that each knight had decorated with a symbol and a motto explaining his purpose for participating in the tournament. Knights hoped to win the tournament, and by so doing, win honor and the hand of Thaisa in marriage. Pericles hoped to improve his fortunes by winning the tournament.

"Which, to preserve my honor, I'll perform," Thaisa replied.

Six knights were participating in the tournament. Five of the knights had a page who held up the knight's small shield so that the King and his daughter could see it.

Simonides asked, "Who is the first who presents himself?"

"A knight of Sparta, my renowned father," Thaisa said, "and the device he bears upon his shield is a black-skinned Ethiopian reaching at the sun. His motto is '*Lux tua vita mihi.*'"

Lux tua vita mihi is Latin for "Your light is life to me."

Simonides said, "He loves you well who believes his life is dependent on you."

King Simonides asked, "Who is the second knight who presents himself?"

"A Prince of Macedon, my royal father, and the symbol he bears upon his shield is an armed knight who has been conquered by a lady. His motto in … Spanish? … is '*Piu por dulzura que por fuerza*.'"

Simonides did not comment on this motto because neither he nor his daughter could translate it.

The motto was a garbled mixture of Italian and Spanish and perhaps one or more other languages and means, roughly, "More by gentleness than by force."

The way Thaisa had conquered this knight and made him love her was through her gentleness.

Although the knight was from Macedon and would have been expected to have a motto in either Latin or his native language, he had tried to impress King Simonides and Thaisa with his knowledge of foreign languages. Unfortunately, his knowledge of foreign languages was lacking. Perhaps, so was his knowledge of Latin.

Simonides asked, "And who is the third knight?"

"The third knight comes from Antioch, and his symbol is a wreath of chivalry. His motto is '*Me pompae provexit apex*.'"

A wreath of chivalry is a wreath worn as a crown by a victor.

The Latin motto, translated literally, is "The peak of the tournament leads me forth." It means "The honor of the tournament brings me here."

"Who is the fourth knight?" Simonides asked.

"One whose shield bears the symbol of a burning torch that's turned upside down. The motto is '*Quod me alit, me extinguit*.'"

The Latin motto means "What inflames me, extinguishes me."

Wax will put a torch out when the torch is held upside down because the wax will melt and run down the torch and extinguish the flame.

Another — bawdy — interpretation was that what inflamed the knight would kill him. Thaisa inflamed the knight, and if the knight won the tournament he would marry Thaisa and "die" in her arms. In this society, "to die" was slang for "to have an orgasm."

Simonides' interpretation was this: "It shows that beauty has its own power and will, which can as well inflame as it can kill."

The fifth knight appeared and Thaisa said, "The symbol of the shield of the fifth knight is a hand surrounded by clouds, holding out gold that has been tested with a touchstone. The motto is '*Sic spectanda fides*.'"

A touchstone is a piece of black quartz. To test the purity of gold, the gold would be rubbed on the touchstone. The mark it left behind told how pure it was. The touchstone came to be a symbol of faithfulness.

The Latin motto meants "Thus faithfulness is tested."

Now the sixth knight — Pericles, clad in rusty armor — arrived.

Simonides asked, "And who is the sixth and last knight, who himself presents his shield with such a graceful courtesy because he has no page?"

Thaisa replied, "He seems to be a stranger, a foreigner, but his symbol is a withered branch that's green only at the top. The motto is '*In hac spe vivo*.'"

The Latin motto mean "In this hope I live."

Simonides said, "This is a pretty moral. From the dejected state he is in, he hopes that by winning you his fortunes yet may flourish."

The first lord said, "I hope that his inward intentions are better than his outward show, which can hardly recommend him. Judging by his rusty exterior, he appears to have practiced more the whipstock than the lance. He seems to be more experienced at using a whip as a driver of a cart than using a lance as a knight in a tournament."

The second lord said, "He well may be a foreigner, for he has come strangely equipped to an honorable tournament."

The third lord said, "He must have let his armor rust on purpose just so he could scour it in the dust in this tournament."

The three lords were judging the knight by the rusty armor he was wearing.

Simonides was a better man than that. He said, "This way of forming an opinion is that of a fool. A fool will scan the outward clothing and think that he is seeing the inward man.

"But wait, the knights are coming into the lists. We will go now and watch the tournament."

They left.

Soon, lots of people shouted, "The badly armored knight!"

Pericles had scored a great victory in the tournament.

<h1 style="text-align:center">— 2.3 —</h1>

In a hall of state was a banquet that was being served after the tournament. Among those present were King Simonides, Thaisa, lords, and attendants. Also present, of course, were the knights who had participated in the tournament. So were a number of ladies.

King Simonides said, "Knights, to say you're welcome is unnecessary. And I need not praise your deeds of valor today because they speak for themselves. I need not be the title page of a book about your deeds — a title page that praises the worth of the book. That would be more than you expect, or more than is fit, since, as I said, every worthy deed of valor commends itself. Prepare to be mirthful, for mirth becomes a feast. You are Princes and my guests."

Thaisa said to Pericles, "But you are my knight and guest. To you I give this wreath of victory, and I crown you King of this day's happiness."

She placed a wreath on his head.

"My success in the tournament came more by luck, lady, than by merit," Pericles said modestly.

"Call it by what you will, the day is yours," King Simonides said to Pericles. "You are the victor, and here, I hope, is no one who envies your success.

"In fashioning an artist, art has thus decreed to make some good, but others to exceed. She makes some good, and some better. She has labored to make you into a scholar."

He said to Thaisa, "Come, Queen of the feast — for, daughter, so you are — here take your place."

He then said, "Marshal, show the others to their places, according to their status."

The knights said, "We are much honored by good Simonides."

"Your presence gladdens our days," Simonides replied. "We love honor; whoever hates honor hates the gods above."

The Marshal showed Pericles the seat of honor and said, "Sir, yonder is your place."

"Some other knight is more fitting to sit here," Pericles said modestly.

The first knight said, "Don't argue, sir; for we are gentlemen who neither in our hearts nor with outward eyes envy the great or despise the low."

Pericles was both high and low. He was the Prince of Tyre, yet he was wearing rusty armor.

He replied, "You are right courteous knights."

"Sit, sir, sit," Simonides said.

He thought, *By Jove, who is King of thoughts, I wonder how it is that I lose my appetite for the delicacies before me when I think about the knight in rusty armor.*

He was so impressed with the tournament's victor, despite his rusty armor, that when he thought about the knight in rusty armor's virtues, he did not feel like eating. Partly, he was wondering what his daughter thought about the knight in rusty armor, and partly, he was wondering if it was a good idea to marry his daughter, a Princess, to someone who apparently lacked material resources and was forced to wear rusty armor.

Thaisa thought, *By Juno, who is Queen of marriage, all the food I eat seems tasteless. I wish that the knight in rusty armor were my meat — my mate.*

She said out loud to her father, "It is certain that the knight in rusty armor is a gallant gentleman."

Simonides replied, "He's only a country gentleman; he has done no more than other knights have done. He has broken a spear or two, so let it pass."

Thaisa thought, *To me the knight in rusty armor seems like a diamond compared to glass.*

Pericles looked at King Simonides and thought, *Yonder King seems to me very much like my father's picture. The picture tells me about that glory that he once had. Princes used to sit, like stars, around his throne, and my father was the Sun for them to revere. All who beheld him were like lesser lights, and they lowered their crowns to acknowledge his supremacy. Whereas now his son — me — is like a glowworm in the night; the glowworm has fire in darkness, but none in light. By this I see that Time is the King of men. Time is their parent and their grave, and he gives them what he will, not what they crave.*

"Are you merry, knights?" King Simonides asked.

A knight replied, "Who can be other than merry in this royal presence and at this feast?"

"Here," Simonides said. "With a cup that's filled to the brim — it is filled as full as you are filled with love for a woman, if you are in love — we drink this health, aka toast, to you."

The knights replied, "We thank your grace."

"Yet wait a moment," Simonides said, looking at Pericles. "Yonder knight sits too melancholy, as if the entertainment in our court lacked a show that might equal his worth."

Simonides was still worried about marrying his daughter to a country gentleman — someone of high enough status to be a knight, but nevertheless lacking in manners. Pericles was in fact lacking in manners. At a banquet, good manners require that a guest enjoy himself — or at least fake it. However, Simonides was a good host and rather than blaming Pericles for not having a good time, he decided to make more of an effort to entertain him.

"Do you notice that the knight in rusty armor is melancholy, Thaisa?" he asked.

"What is that to me, my father?" she replied.

Father and daughter were wondering how the other felt about the knight in rusty armor. Neither was willing to reveal how he or she felt until he or she knew more about how the other felt.

"Listen carefully, my daughter," Simonides said. "Princes in this world should live like the gods above, who freely give to everyone who comes to honor them. Princes who do not do that are similar to gnats, which make a sound, but when they are killed, they are wondered at — how can something so tiny be so annoying?

"The knight honored us by participating in our tournament, and we gave him and the other knights a banquet, but he is not responding as we want — he is not having a good time.

"Let's try to make him have a good time. To make his presence at this banquet sweeter, tell him that we drink this ceremonial bowl of wine to him."

"My father, it is not suitable for me to be so bold to a strange and foreign knight," Thaisa objected. "He may regard as offensive what I say to him, since some men take women's gifts for impudence."

Thaisa wanted to behave as a maiden of good reputation; she could not do so by being forward, although she was attracted to the knight with rusty armor.

Simonides believed that maidens of good reputation obeyed their father.

"What!" Simonides said. "Do as I tell you, or you'll anger me."

Thaisa thought, *Now, by the gods, I can obey his order without harming my reputation. His order could not better please me.*

Using the royal plural, Simonides added, "And furthermore tell him that we desire to know from him where he came from and what is his name and parentage."

Thaisa went to Pericles and said, "The King my father, sir, has drunk to you —"

"I thank him," he replied.

"— wishing that it would enrich your blood."

"I thank both him and you, and I drink his health freely."

Thaisa continued, "And furthermore he desires to know from you where you have come from, your name, and your parentage."

"I am a gentleman of Tyre; my name is Pericles. My education has been in liberal arts and arms. While looking for adventures in the world, I was by the rough seas bereft of ships and men, and after being shipwrecked, I was driven upon this shore."

Pericles did not say that he was the Prince of Tyre. A knight from Antioch was present, and Pericles did not want to reveal everything about himself.

Thaisa returned to her father and said, "He thanks your grace; his name is Pericles, and he is a gentleman of Tyre, who only by misfortune of the seas became bereft of ships and men and was cast on this shore.'

This information relieved Simonides. Pericles was not a country gentleman; Tyre was a notable city. And Pericles had been rich but had suffered misfortune. Also, his misfortune was a good reason for his being melancholy at the banquet.

"Now, by the gods, I pity his misfortune," King Simonides said, "and I will awaken him from his melancholy."

He then said to the knights, "Come, gentlemen, we have sat too long and discussed trifles and wasted the time, which now requires other revels. Your armor, in which you are still dressed, will very well become a soldier's dance. I will hear no excuse, so do not say that this loud music — the clashing of armor as you dance — is too harsh for ladies' heads, since they love men in arms as well as in beds."

The knights, including Pericles, danced.

King Simonides said, "It is good that I asked for the dance, since it was so well performed."

He then said to Pericles, "Come, sir; here is a lady — my daughter — who wants exercise, too. And I have heard that you knights of Tyre are excellent in making ladies trip; and that their measures are as excellent."

King Simonides' words included a — perhaps unintentional — indelicate jest. Ladies who trip are ladies who dance — or ladies who trip and fall sexually. Measures can be rhythmic dance movements — or rhythmic sex movements.

"In those who practice them they are, my lord," Pericles replied.

"You are denying that you are a practiced dancer out of politeness," Simonides said.

The knights and the ladies danced.

The dance of Pericles and Thaisa turned into a dance of courtship, and when the two began dancing too closely, King Simonides said, "Enough! Let go of each other!"

He then said, "I give my thanks, gentlemen, to all; all have done well."

He said to Pericles, "But you have done the best of all."

He referred to both his winning the tournament and what seemed as if it would quickly occur — his winning Thaisa.

King Simonides then ordered, "Pages, bring lights so you can conduct these knights to their different lodgings!"

Using the royal plural, he said to Pericles, "We have given orders for your lodging to be next to our own."

He may have wanted to discourage bed-hopping during the night.

"I am at your grace's pleasure," Pericles said. "I will stay wherever your highness chooses."

King Simonides said, "Princes, it is too late to talk of love; and that's the mark I know you aim at. Certainly, there are ladies enough here for you to aim at. Therefore, each of you go to your rest. Tomorrow you can all do your best to achieve success at love."

Some of the knights may have wanted to pursue Thaisa. Pericles had won the tournament, which made him a clear favorite to marry Thaisa, but it did not necessarily mean that he would marry her. The tournament had been held to celebrate her birthday — not to choose a husband for her.

Helicanus and Escanes spoke together in a room in the governor's house at Tyre. Pericles had given Helicanus authority to govern Tyre in his absence, and Escanes was a loyal lord whom Helicanus respected.

Helicanus said, "No, Escanes, learn this from me. Antiochus from incest lived not free. For this sin, the highest gods did not intend any longer to withhold the vengeance that they had in store. Due to this heinous capital offence, even in the height and pride of all his glory, when he was seated in a chariot of inestimable value, and his daughter was with him, a fire from Heaven came and shriveled up their bodies and made them loathsome. They so stunk that all those eyes that adored them before their fall scorned now that their hands should give them burial."

"It was very strange," Escanes said.

"And yet it was only justice because although this King was great, his greatness was no guard to stop Heaven's arrow — sin had its reward."

"It is very true."

Three lords entered the room.

The first lord said, "See, not a man has influence — either in private conference or public council — with Helicanus except Escanes."

"We shall no longer suffer our grievance in silence," the second lord said. "We shall express our disapproval."

"And cursed be he who will not second it," the third lord said. "We three must put up a united front."

"Follow me, then," the first lord said.

He said loudly, "Lord Helicanus, may we have a word with you?"

"With me?" Helicanus said. "Yes, and welcome. Happy day, my lords."

"Know that our grievances are like a river risen to the top, and now finally they overflow their banks."

"Your grievances?" Helicanus said. "Do not wrong your Prince whom you love."

"Wrong not yourself, then, noble Helicanus," the first lord said. "But if Prince Pericles is alive and in this country, let us greet him, or let us know what ground's made happy by his breath — let us know in which country he is. If he is still alive in the world, we'll seek him out. If he rests in his grave, we'll find him there. We will be resolved that he is still alive and can govern us, or if he is dead, then let us mourn at his funeral and allow us to hold a free election to choose his successor."

"In our opinion, it is most likely that Pericles is dead," the second lord said. "If so, then this kingdom is without a head — and like admirable buildings that are without a roof, it will soon fall to ruin. Therefore, we submit ourselves and make ourselves subjects to your noble self, who best knows how to rule and how to reign. We make you our sovereign."

The three lords shouted, "Live, noble Helicanus!"

"For the sake of honor, withdraw your votes to make me your sovereign," Helicanus said. "If you love and are loyal to Prince Pericles, withdraw your votes. If I were to obey your wish, it would be like I leapt into the seas, where there is an hour's trouble for a minute's ease. Such is the burden of governing as a sovereign — a burden that I do not wish to take on, although as a loyal subject I accepted the responsibility of governing in the Prince's absence. Wait a twelvemonth — one year — longer. Let me persuade you to bear patiently the absence of your King. If he has not returned to Tyre within that year, I shall with aged patience bear your yoke.

"But if I cannot persuade you to be this patient, go and search for him like nobles — like the noble subjects you are — and in your search spend your adventurous worth. Be like the Knights of the Round Table and go on this adventure. If you find Prince Pericles, and if you persuade him to return to Tyre, you shall sit around his crown like diamonds."

"A person is a fool if he will not yield to reason," the first lord said, "and what you have advised us to do is wise."

He said to the other lords, "Since Lord Helicanus has advised us to do this, we will undertake these travels and travails."

Using the royal plural, Helicanus said, "So then, you respect us, and we respect you, and we'll clasp hands. When peers thus knit, a Kingdom ever stands. When nobles are united, their Kingdom stands forever."

— 2.5 —

King Simonides read a letter in a room of his palace at Pentapolis. Some knights entered the room.

The first knight said, "Good morning to the good Simonides."

Simonides said, "Knights, from my daughter I let you know that for the next twelve months she will not undertake a married life. Her reason is known only by herself, and by no means can I get that reason from her."

The second knight asked, "May we get access to her and talk to her, my lord?"

"Indeed, by no means," Simonides replied. "She has so strictly kept herself to her chamber that it is impossible. For twelve moons more she'll wear Diana's livery and remain a virgin and serve the goddess. This by the eye of Cynthia she has vowed and on her virgin honor she will not break it."

Diana was a virgin goddess; she was also a tripartite goddess, and as Cynthia she was the goddess of the Moon.

The third knight said, "Although we are loath to bid farewell, we take our leaves."

The knights exited.

"So, they are well gotten rid of," Simonides said to himself. He was pleased that his lie had worked. "Now to my daughter's letter. She tells me here that either she will wed the foreign knight — Pericles — or she will never again look at day or light.

"It is well, mistress; your choice agrees with mine. I like your choice of husband well. Look how resolute she is in her decision, not caring whether or not I agree with her choice of husband!

"Well, I do commend her choice and will no longer have their match be delayed.

"Quiet! Here he comes: I must pretend that I don't agree with my daughter's choice of him as her husband."

Pericles walked over to King Simonides and said, "All good fortune to the good Simonides!"

"To you as much, sir!" Simonides replied. "I am beholden to you for your sweet music last night. My ears were never better fed with such delightful and pleasing harmony."

"It is your grace's pleasure to praise me," Pericles said. "I do not deserve such high praise."

"Sir, you are music's master."

"I am the worst of all her scholars, my good lord."

"Let me ask you one thing: What do you think of my daughter, sir?"

"She is a very virtuous Princess."

"And she is beautiful, too, isn't she?"

"She is as beautiful as a fair day in summer," Pericles replied. "She is wondrously fair."

"Sir, my daughter thinks very well of you," Simonides said. "Yes, she thinks so well of you that you must be her master, and she will be your scholar. Therefore, be her music master."

"I am unworthy to be her schoolmaster."

"She does not think so," Simonides said. "If you don't believe me, read this letter."

He handed the letter to Pericles, who read it and thought, *What's here? A letter in which she says that she loves me, the knight of Tyre! This must be a cunning trap set by the King to have an excuse to take my life.*

Pericles said out loud to King Simonides, "Seek not to trap me, gracious lord. I am a stranger and a distressed gentleman, who never aimed so high as to love your daughter, but bent all my efforts to honor her."

"You have bewitched my daughter, and you are a villain."

"By the gods, I have not bewitched your daughter," Pericles replied. "Never did any thought of mine intend offence; and never have my actions yet began a deed that might gain her love or cause you to be displeased with me."

"Traitor, you lie," King Simonides said.

"Traitor!"

"Yes, traitor."

"Even in his throat — unless it be the King — anyone who calls me traitor, I return the lie. I say that anyone — except the King — who says that I am a traitor is lying in his throat."

To lie in one's throat is the worst kind of lying.

King Simonides thought, *Now, by the gods, I applaud his courage.*

Pericles said, "My actions are as noble as my thoughts, that never have had a taste of a base descent. I came to your court for the sake of honor, and not to be a rebel to her state. This sword shall prove whoever who thinks otherwise about me is the enemy of honor."

"Is that so?" Simonides said. "Here comes my daughter; she can witness it."

Thaisa walked over to the two men.

Pericles said to her, "Since you are as virtuous as you are beautiful, tell your angry father whether my tongue and hand have ever flirted with you — even a single syllable — or tried to seduce you."

"Why, sir, if you had, who would take offence at something that would make me glad?" Thaisa replied.

"Young lady, are you so determined to have him?" Simonides said.

He thought, *I am glad with all my heart that you are.*

He said out loud to his daughter, "I'll tame you; I'll bring you into subjection. Will you, without having my consent, bestow your love and your affections upon a stranger?"

He thought, *This stranger, for all I know, may have — and I can't think the contrary is true — as noble blood as I have.*

He said, "Therefore listen to me, young lady; either accommodate your will to mine, and you, sir, listen to me, either be ruled by me, or I will make you two — man and wife."

He smiled and said, "Come, your hands and lips must seal your engagement. Kiss each other and shake hands. Good, now that your hands are joined, and you are engaged, I'll destroy your hopes and give you this further 'grief' — I pray that God will give you joy! Are you both pleased?"

Thaisa said to her father, "Yes —"

Then she said to Pericles, "— if you love me, sir."

"I love you as I love my life, and the blood that fosters my life," Pericles replied.

"Are you both agreed that you shall be wed?" Simonides asked.

Both replied, "Yes, if it pleases your majesty."

Simonides replied, "It pleases me so well that I will see you wed and then see with what haste you can get yourselves to bed."

CHAPTER 3
— Prologue —

John Gower said to you the reader, "Now sleep has slaked the drunken revelers at the marriage. No din can be heard except snores throughout the house, snores made louder by the overfed stomachs resulting from this most ceremonious marriage-feast. The cat, with eyes of burning coal — they glow in the dark — now crouches before the mouse's hole, and crickets sing at the oven's mouth, ever the happier because of their dry abode.

"Hymen, god of marriage, has brought the bride to bed, where, by the loss of her maidenhead, a babe is created. Be attentive, and use your fine imaginations to ingeniously augment what you will see in your brain — it will briefly cover what takes a long time in real life.

"What's dumb in show I'll explain with speech."

A dumb show — a show without speaking — appears in your brain, and you see Pericles and Simonides together and a messenger meeting them, kneeling, and giving Pericles a letter. Pericles reads the letter and shows it to King Simonides. The lords kneel to Pericles. Thaisa, pregnant, enters the room, accompanied by Lychorida, a nurse. The King shows Thaisa the letter, and she rejoices. Pericles and Thaisa, accompanied by Lychorida and some attendants, leave King Simonides, who then leaves, accompanied by all who remained.

Gower said, "With many a dark and painstaking journey, a careful search for Pericles is made with all due diligence throughout the four corners of the world. The journeys are made with horses and ships and high expense — whatever can assist the quest.

"At last from Tyre, after reports answered the most foreign and faraway inquiries, to the court of King Simonides a letter is brought. The content of the letter is that Antiochus and his daughter are dead, and that the men of Tyre would like to set the crown of Tyre on the head of Helicanus and make him King, but he immediately resists the mutiny and says to them that if King Pericles does not return home in one year, then he, Helicanus, obedient to their judgments, will take the crown. The gist of this, once brought to Pentapolis, enraptures the regions round about, and everyone applauds and begins to shout, 'Our heir-apparent — Pericles — is a King! Who dreamed, who thought of such a thing?'

"In brief, Pericles must depart from Pentapolis and go to Tyre. His Queen with child makes her desire known — which who shall oppose? She wishes to accompany her husband.

"We omit all their distress and woe.

"Thaisa takes Lychorida, her nurse, and so they go to sea. Their vessel shakes on Neptune's waves; half the flood has their keel cut — they have completed half their voyage. But Lady Fortune's mood changes again; the grisly north wind disgorges such a tempest forth that, like a duck that dives to save its life, so up and down the poor ship drives. The lady shrieks, and because of fear begins to give birth.

"What ensues in this fierce storm you shall read next. I nothing will relate, but the next few pages may conveniently convey the rest better than I can tell it.

"In your imagination see the ship, upon whose deck the sea-tossed Pericles appears and is about to speak."

On board a storm-tossed ship, Pericles said, "Neptune, you god of this great vast sea, rebuke these high waves, which wash both Heaven and Hell. And you, Aeolus, who have command over the winds, call them away from the deep sea, bind them, and keep them behind your brass wall. Jupiter, calm your deafening, dreadful thunders; gently quench your nimble, sulfurous flashes of lightning!"

Pericles' wife, Thaisa, was giving birth. Like other men of the time, he was not present. Understandably, he was worried — childbirth at this time was dangerous.

He called, "Lychorida, how is my Queen doing?"

He then said to the tempest, "You storm, will you maliciously spit all your winds? The seaman's whistle that calls orders to sailors is like a whisper in the ears of a dead person — it is unheard."

He called again, "Lychorida!"

Then he prayed, "Lucina, goddess of childbirth, divinest patroness, and gentle midwife to those who cry at night, convey your deity aboard our dancing boat; make swift the pangs of my Queen's birth-giving! Let her give birth quickly!"

Carrying an infant, Lychorida walked over to Pericles.

"What is the news, Lychorida?" Pericles asked.

"Here is a creature too young for such a place, who, if it had rational understanding, would die, as I am likely to do. Take in your arms this piece of your dead Queen."

The word "piece" has a double meaning. The infant was the Queen's masterpiece; in addition, it was a piece of the Queen — she had given birth to it, and so it carried some of her chromosomes.

Hearing the phrase "dead Queen," Pericles said, "What, Lychorida!"

"Have patience, good sir," Lychorida said. "Be calm. Do not assist the storm by adding your violent emotions to it. Here's all that is left living of your Queen: a little daughter. For the sake of it, be manly, and take comfort in the birth of your daughter."

Pericles, who was not calm, said, "You gods! Why do you make us love your good gifts, and then immediately snatch them away? You gave me Thaisa, and then you took her away from me! We here below do not take back what we give to you — our sacrifices — and therein we treat you honorably."

"Have patience and be calm, good sir," Lychorida said. "Do it for this infant."

Pericles said to his infant daughter, "May the rest of your life be mild! A baby never had a rougher and stormier birth than you. May your life be quiet and gentle. You have had the roughest welcome to this world that any Prince's child has ever had. May what follows be happy and fortunate! You have had as noisy a nativity as fire, air, water, earth, and Heaven can make to herald you from the womb. Even at the beginning of your life your loss — the death of your mother — is more than can be repaid with all you find during your journey through life! Now, may the good gods throw their most propitious eyes upon this infant and its journey!"

Two sailors came over to Pericles.

The first sailor asked Pericles, "What courage do you have, sir? May God save you!"

"I have courage enough," Pericles said. "I do not fear the squall. It has already done to me the worst it can do — it has killed my wife. Yet, because of the love I have for this poor infant, this fresh and new seafarer, I wish that the weather would be quiet."

The first sailor ordered some other sailors, "Slacken the bow-lines there!"

He then shouted at the squall, "You won't be quiet, will you? Then blow, and split yourself!"

The second sailor said, "As long as we have enough sea-room to maneuver and stay away from the rocks, then I don't care if the seawater and spray kiss the Moon."

The first sailor said, "Sir, your Queen must be buried at sea; she must go overboard. The waves are tossed high, the wind is loud, and all will not be calm until the ship is cleared of the dead."

"That's your superstition," Pericles said.

"Pardon us, sir," the first sailor said. "This has been always observed by us sailors at sea, and we strictly observe our traditions. Therefore, quickly yield her corpse to us, for she must go overboard right away."

"Whatever you think is fitting," Pericles said to the sailors.

He then said, "Queen, I am sorry that this is so!"

Lychorida opened the door to the room where Thaisa lay and said to Pericles, "Here she lies, sir."

Pericles said to his wife, "You have had a terrible childbed, my dear. No light, no fire — the rooms in which women give birth are dark. The unfriendly elements forgot you utterly and raged when they should have been quiet. Nor do I have time to give you a proper funeral before you go to your grave, but immediately, with scarcely enough time to put you in a coffin, I must cast you into the sea where you will settle in the ooze at the bottom. There, in place of your tomb and the candles that would burn around your body if you were entombed on land, you will have the spouting whale and turbulent water that must overwhelm your corpse as it lies with simple shells."

Because Pericles thought that there was a chance that the coffin would be driven ashore, he ordered, "Lychorida, tell Nestor to bring me spices to anoint the body, and ink and paper so that I can write a note to put in the coffin. Also tell him to bring me my casket and my jewels. And tell Nicander to bring me the satin coffer."

Pericles wanted to put jewels in the coffin with Thaisa. The casket and the satin coffer would hold the jewels and a document that he intended to write.

He then said, "Now lay the babe upon the pillow by Thaisa.

"Hurry, while I say a priestly farewell to her. Be quick, woman."

Lychorida put down the infant and then exited.

The second sailor said, "Sir, we have a chest beneath the hatches; it is already caulked and sealed with pitch. It is waterproof, and it can serve as her coffin."

"I thank you," Pericles replied. "Mariner, tell me what coast is this?"

"We are near Tarsus," the second sailor said.

"We will go there, gentle mariner, instead of going to Tyre," Pericles said. "Alter the course of this ship. When can we reach it?"

"By break of day, if the wind stops," the second sailor said.

"Then let's make for Tarsus! There I will visit Cleon, for the babe cannot survive the trip to Tyre, and it needs a wet nurse. There I'll leave it so it can be carefully raised. Go to your work, good mariner. I'll bring you the body of my wife soon."

— 3.2 —

Cerimon, a lord of Ephesus, was in a room of his house. With him were two people who were seeking medical help — one for his master. They were wet and cold because they had walked in stormy weather to see Cerimon. It was the morning after the storm, but the weather was still bad.

Cerimon called for his servant: "Philemon, come here!"

Philemon entered the room and said, "Does my lord call?"

"Get fire and food for these suffering men," Cerimon ordered. "It has been a turbulent and stormy night."

Philemon exited.

One of the suffering men said, "I have been in many stormy nights, but such a night as this, until now, I have never endured."

Cerimon said to the man, "Your master will be dead before you return; there's nothing in nature that can be administered to him that can save his life."

Cerimon listened to the second man's heart and then wrote something down, gave it to the man, and said to him, "Give this to the apothecary, and later tell me how it works."

The two men exited. First they would eat and get warm, and then they would leave.

Two gentlemen entered the room.

The first gentleman said, "Good morning."

The second gentleman said, "Good morning to your lordship."

"Gentlemen, why are you up and about so early?" Cerimon asked.

The first gentleman replied, "Sir, our lodgings, standing exposed to the sea, shook as if the earth quaked. The main rafters seemed to break, and it seemed as if the building would topple. Utter surprise and fear made me leave the house."

The second gentleman said, "That is the reason we trouble you so early. It is not because we are eager to get up early and work."

"You say the truth," Cerimon said.

Cerimon was the type to get up early and work hard, but he knew that the two gentlemen were not that type.

The first gentleman said, "I much marvel that your lordship, having rich luxury around you, should at these early hours shake off the golden slumber of repose. It is very strange that human nature should be so acquainted with work when it is not required to work. You have money; you need not work such early hours."

"I have always believed that virtue and skill were endowments greater than nobleness and riches," Cerimon said. "Careless heirs may the latter two — nobleness and riches — darken and expend. Heirs can act ignobly and be spendthrifts. But immortality attends the former two: virtue and skill. These can make a man a god.

"It is known that I have continually studied medicine, through which secret art, by turning over pages written by authorities, I have, together with my personal efforts, made familiar to me and to my aide the blest liquid extracts that dwell in plants, in metals, and in stones. And I can speak of the disturbances that nature works, and of her cures. This gives me more content and more true delight than to be thirsty after tottering, unstable honor, or to tie my treasure up in silken moneybags and please the fool and death. To chase money for the sake of money is the way of the fool, and when we die we can't take our money with us."

The second gentleman said, "Your honor has throughout Ephesus poured forth your charity, and hundreds owe their lives to you because you have restored to them their lives. Not just your knowledge and your personal labor, but also your wallet, which is always open, has built you, Lord Cerimon, such strong renown as time shall never decay."

Two servants carrying a chest entered the room.

The first servant said to the other servant, "Carry it over there."

They moved closer to Cerimon.

"What is that?" Cerimon asked.

The first servant replied, "Sir, just now the sea tossed upon our shore this chest. It is from some shipwreck."

"Set it down, and let's look at it."

Cerimon helped them put the chest down on a table.

The second gentleman said, "It is like a coffin, sir."

"Whatever it is, it is wondrously heavy," Cerimon said. "Wrench the lid open immediately."

The chest was so heavy that he wondered whether it contained gold, so he said, "If the sea's stomach is distressed because it contains too much gold, Lady Fortune does us a good turn by making the sea belch this upon us."

"That is true, my lord," the second gentleman said.

"How tightly it is caulked and smeared with pitch," Cerimon said. "It is waterproof."

Because the chest was so heavy, he asked, although he had already heard the answer, "Did the sea cast it up?"

The first servant replied, "I never saw so huge a billow, sir, as tossed it upon our shore."

"Wrench it open," Cerimon said.

The servants partially opened the chest, and Cerimon said, "Wait! It smells very sweet to me."

"It is a delicate odor," the second gentleman said.

"As delicate an odor as ever hit my nostrils," Cerimon said. "Lift up the lid."

The servants opened the lid, and Cerimon looked inside the chest and said, "Oh, you most powerful gods! What's here! A corpse!"

"Very strange!" the first gentleman said.

"It is shrouded in cloth of state — cloth for royalty," Cerimon said. "It is anointed with full bags of spices — that is what I was smelling! This corpse is safely stored up as if it were in a treasury!"

At this time, spices were very expensive and were kept locked up.

He opened one of the boxes inside the chest and said, "I see a passport, too!"

A passport is a travel document. Corpses travel from the Land of the Living to the Land of the Dead; this passport contained instructions for the disposal of the body.

Cerimon picked up the passport and said, "Apollo, help me to read these words!"

He read the words out loud:

"*Here I give you to understand,*

"*If ever this coffin is driven to land,*

"*I, King Pericles, have lost*

"*This Queen, who is worth all our Earthly treasure.*

"*Whoever finds her, give her a burial.*

"*She was the daughter of a King.*
"*In addition to your keeping this treasure as your fee,*
"*May the gods reward your charity!*"

Inside the chest was Queen Thaisa. Also inside the chest were jewels to pay for her burial.

Cerimon said, "If you still live, Pericles, you have a heart that forever breaks for woe!"

He looked at Thaisa and said, "All this happened last night."

"Most likely, sir," the second gentleman said.

"Not most likely — most certainly," Cerimon said. "It happened last night. Look how fresh she looks! Whoever threw her in the sea were too rough — they did not check her thoroughly enough for signs of life."

He ordered, "Make a fire, and bring here all my boxes in my private room."

A servant left to carry out the order.

Cerimon said, "Death may usurp on nature many hours, and yet the fire of life may kindle again the overwhelmed spirits. I have heard of an Egyptian who had for nine hours lay dead, yet he was revived by good medical care."

The servant returned with boxes and cloths and materials for a fire. The servant, who was competent, knew that cloths would be needed and so had brought them without being asked.

The servant gave Cerimon the boxes and cloths.

"Well done, well done," Cerimon said. "You have brought the fire and cloths."

The servant then left to build a fire in an adjoining room that Cerimon used as a room for patients.

Cerimon said to a second servant, "We need rough and woeful music to help awaken her. Cause it to sound, I ask you."

He rubbed Thaisa's arms as the second servant left to get a viola.

He was annoyed by the second servant's slowness and shouted, "You move like molasses! Faster, blockhead!"

The second servant returned and Cerimon ordered, "Play the music!"

Thaisa began to move, and the gentlemen crowded around her.

Cerimon said, "Please, give her air. Gentlemen, this Queen will live. Nature awakens a warm breath out of her. She has not been in a coma more than five hours. See how she begins to blossom into life's flower again!"

The first gentleman said, "The Heavens, through you, increase our wonder and set up your fame forever. Your fame will never die."

"She is alive," Cerimon said. "Look! Her eyelids, which are cases to those Heavenly jewels — her eyes — that Pericles has lost, begin to part their fringes — her eyelashes — of bright gold. The diamonds — her eyes — of a most praised luster appear, to make the world twice rich. Her eyes are two treasures."

He said to the reviving Thaisa, "Live, and make us weep to hear your fate, fair creature, rare as you seem to be."

Thaisa moved and said, "Dear Diana, goddess, where am I? Where's my lord? What world is this?"

The second gentleman said, "Isn't this strange?"

"It is very rare," the first gentleman replied.

"Hush, my gentle neighbors!" Cerimon said. "Lend me your hands and lift the chest; carry her into the next chamber."

He ordered the second servant, "Get linen."

Then he said, "Now we must take good care of her because if she relapses she will die. Come, come; and may Aesculapius guide us!"

Aesculapius, god of medicine, had been a mortal physician who was capable of bringing the dead back to life.

In a room in Cleon's house were Pericles, Cleon and Dionyza, and Lychorida, who was holding in her arms Pericles' infant daughter.

Pericles said, "Most honored Cleon, I must leave. I had a year to get back to my Kingdom, and my twelve months are expired. Tyre has now an uneasy peace. You, and your lady, receive from my heart all thankfulness! May the gods give you the remaining thanks I owe to you!"

Cleon replied, "Your shafts of fortune, although they hurt you mortally, glance off you and hurt us. You have been badly hurt by the death of your wife; we are also hurt by her death."

"Oh, your sweet Queen!" Dionyza said. "I wish that the strict Fates had allowed you to bring her here, so that our eyes would have been blessed by seeing her!"

"We must obey the gods above," Pericles said. "Even if I would rage and roar as does the sea my wife Thaisa lies in, yet the end must be as it is. My raging and roaring would change nothing. I have named my gentle babe Marina because she was born at sea. Now I turn her over to you and your charity, leaving her as an infant in your care and beseeching you to give her a royal education, so that she may be as well mannered as she is born."

Cleon replied, "Fear not, my lord, but think that your grace, who fed my country with your grain, a good deed for which the people's prayers still fall upon you, must in your child be thought on. We will treat her as we treat you: well and as a savior of ourselves. If I should be so vile as to neglect your infant, the common people, whose famine you relieved, would force me to do my duty. But if I would ever need to be spurred to do my duty, may the gods revenge my neglect of duty upon me and mine, until my descendants die out and no longer exist!"

"I believe you," Pericles replied. "Your honor and your goodness are evidence that make me believe you — you need not vow to me to do your duty."

He said to Dionyza, "I make this vow to my bright Diana, whom we honor: Until my daughter is married, madam, all unscissored shall this hair of mine remain, although I may seem to be willful in making this vow. So I take my leave. Good madam, make me blessed in the care you take in bringing up my child."

Dionyza replied, "I have a daughter myself, who shall not be dearer to me than your daughter, my lord."

"Madam, I give you my thanks and prayers," Pericles said.

"We'll bring your grace to the edge of the shore, and then give you up to the masked Neptune and the gentlest winds of Heaven. Although the sea, the god Neptune's domain, can be dangerous, right now that danger is masked by calm."

"I embrace your offer to accompany me that far," Pericles said.

"Come, dearest madam," he said to Dionyza.

"No tears, Lychorida, no tears," he said to his daughter's nurse, who would stay behind to take care of her. "Look after your little mistress, on whose grace you may depend hereafter. When she is older, she will treat you well."

Pericles said to Cleon, "Come, my lord."

Cerimon and a fully recovered Thaisa were talking in a room in Cerimon's house in Ephesus.

"Madam, this letter, and some jewels, lay with you in your coffin. All of these are yours. Look at the letter. Do you recognize the handwriting?"

"It is my husband's," she replied. "That I was on a ship at sea, I well remember, all the way to the time of giving birth, but whether I delivered my baby at sea, by the holy gods I cannot rightly say. But since King Pericles, my wedded lord, I never shall see again, I will wear the clothing of a chaste vestal votary and never again feel joy."

Thaisa did not remember giving birth. She did not remember what had happened to her husband and her child, if it had been born live, but she felt that they were both dead now. She remembered the storm — terror of the storm had caused her to go into labor early. Due to the ferocity of the storm, a shipwreck seemed certain in these times when travel was very dangerous, and her husband had not been heard from or of. She was so discouraged that she did not want to return to her home or go to her husband's home.

"Madam, if you intend to do that," Cerimon said, "Diana's temple is not far distant. You may live there until your time of death. Moreover, if you please, a niece of mine shall go with you there and serve you."

"My recompense to you is thanks and that's all," Thaisa said. "Yet my good will is great, though the gift of my thanks is small."

CHAPTER 4
— Prologue —

John Gower said to you, the reader, "Imagine that Pericles has arrived at Tyre, where he was welcomed and settled to his own desire. His woeful Queen Thaisa we leave at Ephesus, where she is a votaress to Diana.

"Now to Marina bend your mind, whom our fast-growing — fourteen years have passed — story must find at Tarsus, and by Cleon trained in music and letters. Marina has gained of education all the grace, which makes her both the heart and place of general wonder. People wonder at her great artistry.

"But, alas, that monster envy, which is often the ruin of those who have earned praise, seeks to end Marina's life with the knife of treason.

"This is why:

"King Cleon has one daughter, who is a wench full grown, and is now ripe for the marriage-rite. This maiden is named Philoten, and it is said for certain in our story that she was always with Marina, whether it be when she would weave the finely divided silk with fingers long, slender, and as white as milk, or when she with a sharp needle would wind the cambric cloth, which she improved by hurting — embroidering — it, or when she would sing to the music of the lute and make mute the nightingale, which sings so mournfully, or when she would pen rich and constant verses of homage to her mistress Diana.

"Always this Philoten competes in skill with the perfect Marina. Similarly, a crow might compete with a dove sacred to Venus to see which has whiter feathers.

"Marina gets all the praises, which are paid as debts due to her, and are not given as unearned compliments. In short, Marina's accomplishments outshine all of Philoten's accomplishments.

"Because of this, Queen Dionyza — King Cleon's wife — with exceptional and malicious envy, gets ready a murderer to immediately kill good Marina so that Dionyza's daughter, Philoten, might not be eclipsed by her.

"Because Lychorida, Marina's nurse, is dead, Queen Dionyza is all the easier able to implement her vile thoughts.

"Cursed Dionyza now has the pregnant instrument of wrath impressed to give this blow — that is, she has prepared and made ready the instrument of wrath to give this blow.

"The unborn event — it has not yet happened — I do commend to your attention.

"I can carry winged time only on the lame feet and halting verses of my rhyme. I cannot convey the passage of so much time without the help of your imagination.

"Dionyza now appears, with Leonine, who is a murderer."

Dionyza and Leonine talked together outside near the seashore at Tarsus.

Dionyza said to Leonine, "Remember your oath; you have sworn to murder Marina. It is only a blow, which never shall be known. You cannot do a thing in the world so quickly that will yield you so much profit. Let not conscience, which is cold at first, become inflamed and make you too scrupulous. And don't let pity, which even women have cast off, melt you, but be a soldier to your purpose — be resolute in doing what you have sworn to do."

"I will do it," Leonine said, "but still she is a good and beautiful creature."

"It is all the fitter, then, that the gods should have her," Dionyza replied. "Here she comes weeping for her sole mistress' death — she is weeping because her nurse, Lychorida, died. Are you resolved to kill her?"

"I am resolved."

Marina was picking flowers and putting them in a basket.

She said, "Now I will rob Tellus — Mother Earth — of the flowers that serve as her clothing so that I can use them to strew your grass-covered grave: The yellows, the blues, the purple violets, and the marigolds shall be like a carpet that covers your grave while the days of summer last.

"I am a poor maiden who was born in a tempest when my mother died. This world to me is like a lasting storm, whirling me away from my family."

"How are you, Marina?" Dionyza said. "Why are you alone? How is it that my daughter is not with you? Do not consume your blood with sorrowing."

In this society, people believed that a sorrowful sigh would take a drop of blood away from one's heart.

Dionyza continued, "I will be your nurse now. Lord, how your appearance has changed with this unprofitable woe! Come, give me your flowers. On the seashore, walk with Leonine; the air is invigorating there, and it pierces the body and sharpens the appetite.

"Come, Leonine, take Marina by the arm and walk with her."

"No, thank you," Marina said. "I'll not bereave you of your servant."

Marina, who was bereaved of her nurse, did not want to take Dionyza's servant away from her.

"Come, come," Dionyza said. "I love King Pericles, your father, and yourself with more than foreign heart — I love you two as if I were related to you. We every day expect your father to arrive here. When he shall come and find you, who are regarded as a paragon in all reports about you, thus blighted, he will repent the length of his great voyage, and he will blame both my lord and me and say that we have not taken the best care of you."

Dionyza was evil. She wanted to get rid of Marina, and to do so all she had to do was to wait for Pericles to come and take her away, but she preferred to have Marina murdered.

Dionyza continued, "Go, please. Walk, and be cheerful once again; preserve your excellent complexion, which has stolen the eyes of young and old. You are so pretty that people like to look at you. Don't worry about me. I can go home alone."

"Well, I will go and walk on the seashore with Leonine, yet I don't want to," Marina said.

"Come, come, I know that a walk on the seashore will be good for you," Dionyza said to Marina.

She then said, "Walk half an hour, Leonine, at least. Remember what I have said."

"I do indeed, madam," he replied.

Dionyza said to Marina, "I'll leave you, my sweet lady, for a while. Please, walk slowly so you do not heat your blood. I worry about you."

"I give you my thanks, sweet madam," Marina replied.

Dionyza left.

Marina asked Leonine, "Is this a west wind?"

"South-west," he replied.

"When I was born, there was a north wind."

"Is that so?"

"My nurse told me that my father was never afraid; instead, he shouted, 'Good seaman!' to the sailors as he worked with them, chafing his Kingly hands as he pulled ropes. Clasping the mast, he endured a sea that almost broke the deck."

"When was this?"

"When I was born," Marina said. "Never were waves or wind more violent. From a rope ladder a canvas-climber was washed off a sail into the sea. With black humor, another sailor cried, "Ha! Must you leave us?" Soaked and dripping, they worked hard from stem to stern. The boatswain whistled, and the master called, and all the noise trebled their confusion."

"Come, say your prayers now," Leonine said.

"Why?" Marina asked. "What do you mean?"

"If you require a little time for prayer, I grant it," Leonine said. "Pray, but don't take a long time, for the gods are quick of ear when it comes to hearing prayers, and I am sworn to do my work with haste."

One reason to pray is to make one's peace with God before dying.

Marina asked, "Why are you going to kill me?"

"To satisfy my lady: Queen Dionyza."

"Why would she have me killed? As far as I can remember, truly, I never did anything to hurt her in all my life. I have never spoken a bad word or done an ill turn to any living creature. Believe me, I have never killed a mouse or hurt a fly. If I even stepped unintentionally on a worm, I wept for it. How have I offended her that she believes that my death might be beneficial to her? How have I offended her that she thinks that my life is a danger to her?"

"My commission is not to talk about the deed, but to do it," Leonine replied.

"You will not do it for all the world, I hope," Marina said. "You are good looking, and your looks show that you have a gentle heart. I saw you recently, when you were injured as you parted two who fought. Truly, that good deed showed you in a good light. Do now what you did previously. Your lady seeks my life; come in between us, and save poor me, who is the weaker."

"I have sworn to kill you," Leonine said, "and I will keep my oath."

He grabbed Marina.

Three pirates arrived suddenly.

The first pirate shouted, "Stop, villain!"

Leonine ran away.

Referring to Marina, the second pirate shouted, "A prize! A prize!"

The third pirate said, "Equal shares, mates. We will share this prize equally. Come, let's take her onboard ship immediately."

The three pirates left with Marina as their captive.

Leonine came back. He had not been close enough to hear what the third pirate had said.

"These roguing thieves serve the great pirate Valdes," Leonine said to himself, "and they have seized Marina. Let her go. There's no hope she will return. I'll swear that she's dead and I have thrown her into the sea. But I'll spy further on her and the pirates. Perhaps they will only please themselves upon her and not carry her onboard their ship. If they rape her and then leave her on the seashore, then I will kill her."

A male pandar, a female bawd, and their servant Boult were in a room in their brothel in the city of Mytilene on the island of Lesbos.

"Boult!" Pandar shouted.

"Sir?"

"Search the market closely and see if you can find a woman we can buy. Mytilene is full of gallants who are willing to frequent brothels. We lost too much money this latest market time by being too wenchless. We need another prostitute."

"We were never so much out of creatures," Bawd said. "We have only three prostitutes, who are of poor quality, and they can do no more than they can do, and they with continual action in entertaining customers are just as good as rotten."

"Therefore let's have fresh whores, whatever we pay for them," Pandar said. "If there be not a conscience to be used in every trade, we shall never prosper."

By that, he meant that every business needed to follow ethical business principles. Since he and his wife, Bawd, ran a brothel, they needed to provide good whores in return for good money.

"You say the truth," Bawd said. "It is not our bringing up of poor bastards — as, I think, I have brought up some eleven —"

She meant that ethical business principles meant more than bringing up the bastard children who had been born to the whores.

Bolt interrupted, "— yes, you brought them up to eleven years of age, and then you brought them down again; that is, you made them work in the brothel. But shall I search the market?"

"What else, man?" Bawd said. "The stuff we have, a strong wind will blow it to pieces — these whores are so pitifully sodden."

The whores were sodden because they had spent time soaking in hot tubs as a treatment for venereal disease.

"You say the truth," Pandar said. "They're too unwholesome; they are diseased — my conscience makes me admit that. A Transylvanian lay with the little baggage — one of our whores — and now the poor man is dead."

"Yes, she quickly cheated him: He gave us money and she made him roast-meat — that is, he acquired a venereal disease, roasted himself in hot water, hoping for a medical cure, and then became food for worms," Boult said. "But I'll go search the market."

He left to carry out his errand.

Pandar said, "Three or four thousand chequins — Italian gold coins — would be a pretty good nest egg that would allow us to live quietly, and so stop running a brothel."

"Why should we stop running a brothel, I ask you?" Bawd said. "Is it shameful to make money when we are old?"

"Our reputation is not as good as our profit, and our profit is not good enough to justify the dangerous risks we take," Pandar said. "Therefore, if in our youths we could pick up some pretty fortune and property, it would be a good idea to keep the door to our brothel closed. Besides, the bad relationship we have with the gods is a persuasive reason for us to retire from this line of work."

"Come, other kinds of people offend the gods as well as we," Bawd said.

"As well as we!" Pandar said. "Yes, and better, too; we offend worse. Our profession is not a trade; it's no calling. It is certainly not a religious calling. But here comes Boult."

Boult entered the brothel, with the pirates and Marina following him. Marina was still wearing the clothing of an upper-class woman.

Boult said to Marina, "Come this way."

He then said to the pirates, "My masters, you say that she's a virgin?"

"Sir," the first pirate said, "there is no doubt about it."

Boult said to Pandar, "Master, I have gone through negotiations for this piece — this woman — whom you see. If you like her, good; if not, I have lost my deposit I gave these pirates to bring her here so you could see her and decide whether to buy her."

Bawd asked, "Boult, has she any accomplishments?"

"She is pretty, speaks well, and is wearing excellent clothing. She needs no other accomplishments than these for this line of work."

Bawd asked, "What's her price, Boult?"

"I cannot negotiate a price even a cent lower than a thousand gold coins."

Pandar said to the pirates, "Well, follow me, my masters, you shall have your money at once."

He then said, "Wife, take her under your care; instruct her in what she has to do, so that she may not be raw in her entertainment. She needs to know how to entertain her customers."

Pandar and the pirates went into another room of the brothel where Pandar kept his money.

Bawd ordered, "Boult, note her distinguishing physical characteristics: the color of her hair, complexion, height, and age. Go to the marketplace and describe her and say that her virginity is guaranteed. Cry, 'He who will pay the most money shall have her first.' Such a maidenhead will not sell cheaply, if men still are as they have been in the past. Do this now."

"I shall do it," Boult said as he exited.

Marina said, "I regret that Leonine was so slack — so slow — in doing his duty! He should have struck me down without speaking to me! I regret that these pirates were not barbarous enough! They should have thrown me overboard into the sea so that I could go and seek my mother!"

"Why are you crying, pretty one?" Bawd asked.

"Because I am pretty," Marina replied.

"Come, the gods have done well by you."

"I am not accusing them of anything."

Bawd said, "You have fallen into my hands, and here you are likely to live."

"I blame myself for escaping from the hands of the person who was likely to kill me," Marina replied. "It was very likely that I would die."

"You are likely to die here," Bawd said. "Here you shall live in sexual pleasure."

In the slang of that time and place, "to die" meant "to have an orgasm."

"No," Marina said.

"Yes, indeed you shall," Bawd said, "and you shall taste gentlemen of all fashions. You shall fare well. You shall have the difference of all complexions. You will have sex with men of all kinds and colors. Why are you covering your ears?"

"Are you a woman?"

"If I am not a woman, then what do you think I am?" Bawd asked. "What would you have me be, if I am not a woman?"

"I would have you be an honest — that is, chaste — woman, or no woman at all."

"Darn you, little goose — you greenhorn," Bawd said. "I think you are going to give me some trouble. Come, you're a foolish young sapling, and you must be bent as I would have you. You must do what I tell you to do."

"May the gods defend me!"

"If it pleases the gods to defend you by men, then men must comfort you, men must feed you, men must sexually stir you," Bawd said. "You will make your living by men. Look, Boult's returned."

Boult entered the brothel.

"Now, sir, have you advertised her throughout the marketplace?" Bawd asked.

"I have cried loudly and described her in detail, almost even telling potential customers the number of her hairs. I have drawn her picture with my voice."

"Please tell me what was the reaction of the people, especially of the younger sort?"

"Indeed, they listened to me as they would have listened to their father's last will and testament to see what he had left them. There was a Spaniard whose mouth drooled; he was so taken by my advertisement that he metaphorically went to bed with her description."

"We shall see him here tomorrow with his best clothing on," Bawd said.

"He will be here tonight, tonight," Boult predicted. "But, mistress, do you know the French knight whose legs are unsteady?"

Unsteady legs were a sign of syphilis.

"Who, Monsieur Veroles?" Bawd asked.

The name was derived from the French word for syphilis, so it was as if the Frenchman's name was Mr. Syphilis.

"Yes, he," Boult said. "He attempted to cut a caper — jump in the air and click his heels together — after hearing my proclamation, but he could not and groaned, and he swore that he would see her tomorrow."

"Well, well," Bawd said. "As for him, he brought his disease hither. Here he does but renew it."

Syphilis was known as the French disease. The Frenchman had already been infected with the disease before he entered the brothel; once inside the brothel, he made sure that the disease would not be cured.

Bawd continued, "I know he will come in our shadow — under our roof — to scatter his crowns of the Sun."

French crowns were known as crowns of the Sun; they were gold coins on which the Sun was shown over a depiction of a shield.

"Well, if we had of every nation a traveller, we should lodge them here with this sign," Boult said, motioning to Marina.

He meant that every traveler would want to have sex with Marina.

Bawd said to Marina, "Please, come here for awhile. You have a fortune coming to you. You will make a lot of money. Listen to me: You must seem to do that fearfully which you commit willingly, and you must seem to despise profit where you have most gain. You must pretend to cry because you live as you do — as a prostitute. You must pretend to hate being a prostitute. If you do that, your lovers will pity you and give you money. It is seldom in life that pity will give you a good reputation and that a good reputation will make a good profit."

"I don't understand what you are saying," Marina said.

"Take her home, mistress, and speak plainly to her," Boult said. "These blushes of hers must be quenched with some immediate practice."

"You say the truth, indeed," Bawd said. "These blushes of hers must be quenched. Brides go to do the act with shameful blushes although the brides are allowed to do the act by law. Brides blush, but they do the act."

"Some brides blush, and some do not," Boult said. "But, mistress, since I have bargained for the joint —"

Bawd, who knew what he wanted, said, "— you may cut a morsel off the spit."

Pandar, Bawd, and Boult all regarded the prostitutes as merchandise rather than full human beings. To them, prostitutes were creatures and stuff and pieces, and now a piece of roast meat. Certainly, Marina was a piece — a masterpiece of virtue, not the piece of ass they thought she was.

Bawd would allow Boult to have sex with Marina — after her virginity had been sold.

"I have permission, then?" Boult asked.

"Who would deny you permission?" Bawd replied.

She said to Marina, "Come, young one, I like your clothing well."

Boult said, "Yes, indeed. Her clothing shall not be changed yet."

He meant that soon enough Marina would wear the clothing of a prostitute, but for now her fine clothing increased her price.

Bawd gave Boult some money and said, "Boult, spend that in the town. Tell everyone what a guest we have here. You'll lose nothing by men visiting our guest because you shall earn some tips.

"When nature formed this piece, she meant you a good turn. You will make some money from this piece and have a turn with her in bed. Therefore, tell everyone what a paragon of beauty she is, and you will make a profit out of your advertising."

"I tell you, mistress, thunder shall not so awaken the eels in their muddy beds as my describing her beauty shall stir up the trouser-snakes of the lewdly inclined," Boult said. "I'll bring home some customers tonight."

Boult exited.

"Come," Bawd said to Marina, "and follow me."

"If fires are hot, knives sharp, or waters deep, untried I still my virgin knot will keep," Marina said.

She meant that she would commit suicide if that was what it took for her to remain a virgin.

She then said, "Diana, virgin goddess, aid me and help me keep my virginity!"

"What have we to do with Diana?" Bawd asked, amused. "Please, come with me."

Cleon and Dionyza were talking together in a room of their palace.

"Are you foolish?" Dionyza asked. "Can the murder be undone?"

"Oh, Dionyza, the Sun and Moon have never looked upon such a piece of slaughter!"

"I think you'll turn into a child again," Dionyza said. "You're acting like a baby."

"Were I the chief lord of all this spacious world, I would give all this spacious world to undo the deed," Cleon said. "Marina was a lady much less in blood than virtue. She was much more virtuous than she was noble, and yet she was a Princess whose crown would equal any single crown of the Earth in a fair and just comparison! Leonine, who was a villain, you have poisoned. If you had drunk the poison as a toast to him, it would have been a kindness — much better than the deeds you have actually committed. What will you say when noble Pericles returns to claim his child?"

"I will say that she is dead. Nurses are not the Fates. They don't control death. They can try to foster a child so that it will live and grow up, and yet they do not always have the power to keep the child alive.

"Marina died at night — that is what I'll say. Who can contradict it? No one, unless you play the pious innocent, and in order to acquire a reputation for honesty, cry out, 'She died by foul play.'"

"I won't do that," Cleon said. "Well, well, of all the sins beneath the Heavens, the gods like this one the worst."

"Be one of those who think the petty wrens of Tarsus will fly away from here, and reveal this crime to Pericles," Dionyza said.

In folktales and ballads, birds sometimes communicated information about a person who had committed a murder. Such stories may have had their origin in this ancient tale: Robbers murdered the ancient Greek poet Ibykos (who lived in the 6th century B.C.E.). Before dying, he exclaimed to the robbers that some birds — cranes — nearby would be his avengers. The robbers laughed at him. When the robbers later entered a city, one of the robbers saw some cranes and shouted, "Look — the avengers of Ibykos." This aroused the curiosity of the citizens of the city, who — after investigating and discovering that the robbers had murdered Ibykos — put the robbers to death.

Cleon said, "Whoever simply adds his approval after the fact to such an evil proceeding as a murder like this, although he did not give consent before the murder occurred, does not flow from honorable sources. His ancestors cannot be noble people."

In this society, people believed that nobility was a result of the honorable deeds of one's ancestors.

"Be it so, then," Dionyza said. "Yet no one, except you, knows how she came to be dead. No one knows, since Leonine is gone.

"Marina overshadowed my daughter, and Marina stood between my daughter and her fortunes. No one would look at my daughter; instead, they cast their gazes on Marina's face, while our daughter was scorned and regarded as a drab not worth the time of day — people did not even regard her as worth a greeting when they met her.

"This treatment of our daughter pierced me through, and though you call my course of action unnatural — in which case you do not much love your daughter — yet I find that my course of action is an enterprise of kindness that I have done for the benefit of your only daughter."

Cleon replied, "May the Heavens forgive what you have done!"

Dionyza said, "As for Pericles, what can he say? We wept as we followed Marina's hearse, and we still continue to mourn. Her tomb is almost finished, and her epitaphs in glittering golden letters express a widely made praise of her, and it shows that we care about her since the tomb is being built at our expense."

"You are like the Harpy, which has the face of a woman and the wings and talons of an eagle," Cleon said. "In order to betray others, you deceive them with your angel's face and then seize them with your eagle's talons."

"You are like a person who superstitiously swears to the gods that winter kills the flies," Dionyza replied. "You are so afraid of the gods that you fear them blaming you for the death of flies at the coming of winter. But I know you'll do as I advise — you'll keep this murder secret."

Standing in front of Marina's tomb, John Gower said to you the reader, "We make time pass quickly, and we make the longest distances short. We sail the seas in mussel shells, if we wish to. We make the wish to travel, and then our imagination takes us from boundary to boundary, region to region. Our imagination allows us to travel quickly wherever we want to go.

"Pardon me, but we commit no crime when we use one language in each of the several lands where our scenes are set.

"Please learn from me, who stand in the gaps of our story so that I can teach you the stages of our story — my job is to fill in the gaps. Pericles is now again traversing the hostile seas, attended by many a lord and knight, so that he can see his daughter, who is all his life's delight.

"Old Escanes, whom Helicanus recently advanced to great and high rank and status, has been left behind to govern Tyre. Bear in mind that old Helicanus sails along with Pericles.

"Well-sailing ships and bounteous winds have brought King Pericles to Tarsus — your thought is his pilot, and so your thoughts shall steer his ship — so that he can fetch his daughter home, but she has already left Tarsus.

"Now see in your mind some of our characters move awhile like shadows and motes of dust dancing in Sunlight. I will tell you what is going on so that your ears will understand what your mind's eyes are seeing."

A dumb show — a show without speaking — appears in your brain, where you see Pericles and his train of attendants arrive at Tarsus. Cleon and Dionyza meet him and show him the tomb of Marina. Pericles mourns, puts on sackcloth, and departs with much grief.

Gower said, "See how belief may suffer by foul show! The hypocritical acting of Cleon and Dionyza makes Pericles mourn. The pretended passion of Cleon and Dionyza stands in for truly felt woe, and Pericles is all devoured with sorrow, with sighs shot through his body, and the biggest tears shower his body.

"Pericles leaves Tarsus and again embarks on a journey. Previously, he had sworn never to cut his hair until his daughter was married. Thinking that now his daughter will never be married, he vows never to wash his face, and never to cut his hair. He puts on sackcloth, and he goes to sea. He carries inside himself a tempest, which tears his mortal vessel — his body — and yet he rides it out.

"Now please know that the following epitaph was written for Marina by wicked Dionyza."

He read this inscription that was written on Marina's tomb:

"The fairest, sweetest, and best lies here,

"Who withered in her spring of year.

"She was the King of Tyre's daughter,

"On whom foul death has made this slaughter.

"Marina was she called; and at her birth,

"Thetis, being proud, swallowed some part of the Earth.

"Therefore the Earth, fearing to be overflowed,

"Has Thetis' birth-child on the Heavens bestowed,

"Wherefore she does — and swears she'll never stint —

"Make raging battery upon shores of flint."

Dionyza had made a mistake in the epitaph. Thetis was a sea goddess who was the mother of Achilles, the greatest Greek warrior in the Trojan War. Dionyza had meant to refer to Tethys, the wife of Oceanus, the god of the ocean.

Marina was the birth-child of Tethys because Marina had been born at sea. Tethys was so proud of Marina that the sea swelled with pride and so the sea flooded the seashores. In Dionyza's epitaph for Marina, the land, fearing that it would be completely flooded, had caused Marina to go to Heaven. In retaliation, sea waves continually batter the seashores.

John Gower continued, "No mask becomes black villainy as well as soft and tender flattery.

"Now we will let Pericles believe that his daughter's dead, and Pericles will allow Lady Fortune to determine where he goes.

"But we will visit his daughter and witness her woe and heavy grief in her unholy service as a prostitute. Have patience, then, and think that you now are all in Mytilene. If you think you are there, you will be there."

Two gentlemen came out of the brothel in Mytilene.

The first gentleman asked, "Did you ever hear the like?"

The second gentleman replied, "No, I never have, and I never shall again in such a place as this, once she — Marina — has gone."

"To have divinity preached there! In a brothel! Did you ever dream of such a thing?

"No, no. Come, I am for no more bawdy houses. I want nothing more to do with brothels. Shall we go and hear the vestal priestesses sing?"

"I'll do anything now that is virtuous, but I am out of the way of rutting forever. No more unethical sex for me!"

— 4.6 —

In a room of the brothel, Pandar, Bawd, and Boult talked about Marina.

"I would pay twice what I paid for her if it meant that she never would have come here," Pandar said.

"Darn her!" Bawd said. "She's able to freeze the god Priapus, and undo a whole — as well as hole — generation."

Priapus was the male god of fertility, and his idols depicted him with a huge erection. Cold results in shrinkage, and freezing cold results in lack of erections. Marina was so talented at not losing her virginity that she could freeze Priapus and so prevent a new generation of children from being born.

Bawd continued, "We must get Marina to lose her virginity. We must either get her ravished — rape is what I mean — or get rid of her."

The phrase "to ravish" is odd. One meaning is "to rape"; another meaning is "to fill with delight."

Bawd continued, "When Marina is supposed to do for clients what prostitutes are supposed to do and show them the kindness of our profession, she instead has her quirks, her reasons, her master reasons, her prayers, and her knees."

One of Marina's "quirks" was an unwillingness to be forced to have sex for the financial improvement of Pandar, Bawd, and Boult.

Bawd continued, "Marina would make a Puritan of the Devil if he should ever attempt to buy a kiss from her."

Boult said, "Indeed, I must rape her, or she'll disfurnish us of all our cavaliers, and make our swearers priests. We will lose all our customers because she will make them virtuous."

Pandar said, "I wish that the pox — syphilis — would fall upon her greensickness for me!"

Maidens sometimes suffered from greensickness when they reached puberty. People of the time felt that the sickness resulted from unrequited love. If the love were requited — cynical people might say, with a roll in the hay — the sickness would be cured.

Bawd said, "Indeed, there's no way to be rid of greensickness except by the way that leads to the pox."

She heard a noise, looked up, and said, "Here comes the Lord Lysimachus; he is disguised."

Boult said, "We should have both lord and lower-down, high-class and low-class, if the peevish baggage would just give way to customers. If she would just do what a prostitute is supposed to do, she would be a very successful prostitute."

Lysimachus said, "How is everyone?" and then he joked, "How much does it cost to buy a dozen virginities?"

"Now, may the gods thoroughly bless your honor!" Bawd said.

"I am glad to see that your honor is in good health," Boult said.

Anyone interested in deflowering a dozen virgins must be in good health.

"You may be glad indeed," Lysimachus replied. "It is better for you if your customers stand upon sound legs. If their legs are unsteady, they may have the pox — and may have gotten it here! What wholesome iniquity do you have that a man may deal with, and yet defy the surgeon? Do you have a healthy whore I can sleep with and not have to see a doctor later?"

Bawd replied, "We have here one, sir, if she would — but there never came her like in Mytilene."

"If she would do the deed of darkness, you would say," Lysimachus said. "That is what you were going to say, right?"

"Your honor knows well enough what I was going to say."

"Well, call her forth, call her forth."

Pandar left to get Marina.

Boult said, "Flesh and blood, sir, are white and red. When you see her, you shall see a rose; and she were a rose indeed, if she had but —"

He stopped.

Lysimachus knew the proverb: No rose is without a thorn — that is, a prick. He also knew that the word "rose" was slang for "vagina."

"If she had but what?" he asked.

"Sir, I can be modest," Boult replied.

"Modesty dignifies the reputation of a bawd, no less than it gives a good report to a member to be chaste," Lysimachus said.

He meant that modesty was as useful to a bawd or a pandar as it is to a male member, aka penis.

Pandar returned with Marina.

Bawd said, "Here comes that which still grows attached to the stalk; this rose has never yet been plucked, I can assure you. Isn't she a beautiful creature?"

"Indeed, she would serve after a long voyage at sea. A sex-starved sailor would love to have a go at her. Well, there's some money for you. Leave us."

"I ask your honor to give me permission to say a word to her," Bawd said. "I'll be done quickly."

"I give you permission, but be quick."

Bawd said privately to Marina, "First, I would have you note that this man is an honorable man."

By "honorable," Bawd meant "high-ranking." By "note," she meant "know."

Marina replied, "I hope to find him honorable, so that I may worthily note him."

By "honorable," Marina meant "virtuous." By "worthily note," she meant "treat him with respect."

"Next, I want you to know that he's the governor of this country, and a man to whom I am bound," Bawd said.

She was bound to him because he had not shut down her brothel.

"If he governs the country, you are bound to him indeed — you are a citizen of his country and you should be a good citizen. However, I don't know how honorable he is as governor."

"Please tell me, without any more virginal fencing — without any fencing with words to guard your virginity — will you treat him kindly? He will line your apron with gold."

Women in some professions can lift their aprons and catch money in them. The lifting of the aprons — and other articles of clothing — can result in financial gain.

"What he will do graciously, charitably, and like a gentleman, I will thankfully receive."

Bawd lifted her eyes to the Heavens.

Impatient, Lysimachus asked, "Are you done yet?"

Bawd replied, "My lord, she's not paced yet. She has not been broken in. You must take some pains to work her so that she will do what you want her to do."

She was referring to Marina as if she were a horse that needed to be broken and trained.

She then said to Pandar and Boult, "Come, we will leave his honor and her together. Let's go."

Pandar, Bawd, and Boult exited.

Lysimachus was cynical; he doubted that Marina was a virgin. Therefore, he said to her, "Now, pretty one, how long have you been at this trade?"

"What trade, sir?"

"Why, I cannot name it without causing offense."

The trade Lysimachus meant was prostitution, but Marina now interpreted the word "trade" as meaning "way of life." Her way of life was being a virgin.

"I cannot be offended by my trade," Marina said. "Please name it."

"How long have you been of this profession?"

The profession that Lysimachus meant was prostitution, but Marina now interpreted the word "profession" as meaning "character or nature." Again, she was a virgin.

"Ever since I can remember," she replied.

"Did you go to it so young? Were you a gamester at five or at seven?" Lysimachus asked.

Lysimachus was using "go to it" to mean "to have sex," and he was using "gamester" to mean "prostitute."

A gamester plays a game, and Marina knew that she was a virginal player in the game of life.

"Earlier, too, sir, if now I be one," Marina said.

Thinking that there was no "if" about it, Lysimachus said, "Why, the house you dwell in proclaims you to be a creature of sale."

A creature of sale is a prostitute.

"Do you know this house to be a place of such entertainment, and yet you will come into it?" Marina said. "I have heard that you are a man of honorable qualities and that you are the governor of this place."

"Why, has your principal told you who I am?"

A principal is a manager or superior.

"Who is my principal?" Marina asked.

"Why, your herb-woman," Lysimachus replied. "She plants seeds and roots of shame and iniquity. She helps men to plant their seeds — their semen. Oh, you have heard something of my power, and so you stand aloof for more serious wooing. You want a long-term relationship with me. But I protest to you, pretty one, my authority shall either not see you, or else it will look friendly upon you. I will not use my power to hurt you as you practice your profession. I will either ignore you or perhaps even help you. Now take me to some private place with a bed. I am impatient."

"If you were born to honor, show it now. Act like the honorable man you are," Marina said. "If you have acquired the reputation of being honorable, then show that the judgment is good that thought you worthy of it. By acting honorably, you can show that you deserve your reputation of being an honorable person."

"What's this? What's this?" Lysimachus said. He was impressed by Marina's words. "Speak some more; be sage. Speak wisdom."

"I am a maiden, although most ungentle fortune has placed me in this pigsty, where, since I came here, venereal diseases have been sold for a higher price than medicine. I wish that the gods would set me free from this unhallowed place even if it meant that they would transform me into the humblest bird that flies in the pure air!"

In Ovid's *Metamorphoses*, the gods sometimes transform maidens such as Daphne and Syrinx into other beings such a laurel tree or a bed of reeds to help them escape rape. In one story, Neptune pursued a virgin named Cornix as he tried to rape her. Minerva, a virgin goddess, pitied the girl and transformed her into a crow. John Gower wrote about her escape in his *Confessio Amantis*.

Like other lecherous men to whom Marina had spoken, Lysimachus reformed. He was embarrassed about his lechery, and he now tried to deny that he had been lecherous.

"I did not think you could have spoken so well," Lysimachus said. "I never dreamed that you could. Had I brought here a corrupted mind, your speech would have altered it. Wait, here's gold for you. Persevere in that clear way you are going, and may the gods strengthen you!"

"May the good gods preserve you!" Marina replied.

"As for me, think that I came here with no ill intent because to me even the doors and windows here stink vilely. Fare you well. You are a masterpiece of virtue, and I doubt not that your training has been noble.

"Wait, here's more gold for you. A curse upon that man — may he die like a thief! — who robs you of your goodness! If you ever again hear from me, it shall be for your good."

Lysimachus opened the door to exit. Boult, who was standing outside the door, said, "I beg your honor, give me a tip — one coin."

"Get away from me, you damned doorkeeper!" Lysimachus said.

Boult did keep the door. Part of his job was to stand outside the door until the john had finished doing the deed with the whore.

Lysimachus said, "Your house, except for this virgin who props it up, would fall and bury you. Get away from me!"

He exited, and Boult entered the room.

"What's this?" he said to Marina. "We must take another course of action with you. If your obstinate and perverse chastity, which is not worth a breakfast in the cheapest country under the sky, shall ruin a whole household, then let me be gelded like a cocker spaniel. Come with me."

"Where are you taking me?" Marina asked. "What do you want with me?"

"I must have your maidenhead taken off, and if I don't, I'll make sure that the common hangman executes your maiden's head," Boult said. "I am going to take your virginity away from you. Come with me. We'll have no more gentlemen driven away. Instead, you shall do your duty like other whores. Come with me, I say."

Bawd entered the room and said, "What's going on? What's the matter?"

"Things get worse and worse, mistress," Boult said. "Marina has spoken holy words to the Lord Lysimachus."

"How abominable!" Bawd said.

"She makes our profession out to be one that would stink before the face of the gods."

"Hang her up at the end of a rope forever!"

"The nobleman would have dealt with her like a nobleman and tipped well, but she sent him away as cold as a snowball," Boult said. "He was saying his prayers, too."

"Boult, take her away," Bawd said. "Use her at your pleasure; do what you want with her. Crack the glass of her virginity. Break her hymen, and make the rest malleable. Once she ceases to be a virgin, she will become a whore."

"Even if she were a thornier piece of ground than she is, she shall be plowed," Boult said.

Plowing this particular ground sometimes results in the crop of a baby.

"Pay attention, you gods!" Marina cried.

"She conjures!" Bawd said. "She is calling for supernatural help! Away with her! I wish that she had never come within my doors!"

She said to Marina, "May you be hanged!"

She said to Boult, "She was born to ruin us."

She said to Marina, "Will you not go the way of womankind? At one point or another, women cease to be virgins! Accept it, you fancy dish of chastity with rosemary and bay leaves!"

To Bawd, Mariana was a dish — an object — to be consumed.

Bawd exited.

"Come, mistress," Boult said to Marina. "Come with me."

"What do you want with me?"

"I want to take from you the jewel — your virginity — that you hold so dear."

"Please, tell me one thing first."

"I am thinking about your one thing."

In this culture, "thing" was slang for genitals.

Marina asked, "What can you wish your enemy to be?"

"Why, I could wish my enemy to be my master, or rather, my mistress," Boult replied.

He meant that if his enemy should be his master or, better, his mistress, then he would have no enemy because his enemy would be his friend.

"Neither of these — master nor mistress — are as bad as you are; they better you by giving you a job. In addition, they are better than you since they have an advantage over you because you are in their command — they give you orders.

"However, although they benefit you by giving you a job, you hold a position for which the most tortured fiend of Hell would not exchange places with you for fear of hurting its reputation. You are the damned doorkeeper to every scoundrel who comes here looking for a whore. Your ear is liable to be pounded by the angry fist of every rogue. Your food has been belched on by infected lungs."

"What would you have me do?" Boult asked. "Would you have me go to the wars where a man may serve seven years and lose a leg, and not have money enough in the end to buy himself a wooden one?"

"Do anything except what you do now," Marina said. "Empty filth from old receptacles such as sewers and use the common shores to remove it."

The common shores were places on the seashore where the general public was allowed to put filth to be swept out to sea at high tide. Boult's job would be to remove sewage by placing it on the common shores.

Marina continued, "Serve as an apprentice to the common hangman. Any of these ways of making a living are better than this job that you are doing now. If a baboon could speak, he would say that he would not do your job because it would lower his reputation. I wish that the gods would safely deliver me from this place!

"Here, here's gold for you. If you want to benefit your master, proclaim in the marketplace that I can sing, weave, sew, and dance. I have other virtues that I'll keep myself from boasting about. Say that I will undertake to teach all these. I don't doubt that this populous city will yield many scholars. I am sure that this city has many pupils whom I can teach for money."

"But can you teach all these things that you speak of?" Boult asked.

"If you prove that I cannot, then take me into your home — this brothel — again, and prostitute me to the basest fellow who frequents your house."

"Well, I will see what I can do for you," Boult said. "If I can find a place for you, I will."

"Be sure to find me a place among honest — chaste — women."

"Indeed, my acquaintance lies little among them," Boult said. "I can't say that I know many chaste women. But since my master and mistress have bought you, I can do nothing except with their consent; therefore, I will tell them what you are proposing. I am sure that I shall find them agreeable enough. Come with me, and I'll do for you what I can. Come with me."

CHAPTER 5
— Prologue —

John Gower said to you the reader, "Marina thus escapes from the brothel, and it happens that she comes into an honest house, our story says. She sings like an immortal goddess, and she dances like a goddess to her admirable songs. Learned scholars are struck dumb by her intelligence, and with her needle she embroiders nature's own shapes, whether of bud, bird, branch, or berry, so well that her art seems to be twin sisters of the natural roses. Her linen thread and silk seem to be a twin to the ruby-red cherry, and so she does not lack pupils who are noble. They wish to learn how to embroider as she does and so they pour their bounty on her, and whatever she makes she gives to the cursed bawd.

"Here we leave her, and we turn our thoughts again to her father, where we left him, on the sea. We lost him there, but now, driven before the winds, he has arrived here where his daughter is dwelling, and so suppose him now to be at anchor on this coast.

"The city has been celebrating the sea-god Neptune's annual feast. From that feast, Lysimachus sees the Tyrian ship. Its banners are sable — black — and they are trimmed with rich expense. Lysimachus now hurries to that ship in his barge.

"In your imagination once more put your sight on Pericles, who is sorrowing because he believes that his daughter, Marina, is dead. Imagine his ship and let it take up a big space in your imagination. Soon, much shall be revealed. Sit back, read, and pay attention."

Pericles, who had not washed or cut his hair for months, and who had lost weight, sat on a couch on the deck of his ship in the harbor of Mytilene. A barge had just sailed up to his ship. Standing near Pericles was Helicanus.

Two sailors arrived on deck. One sailor was from Pericles' ship, which was from Tyre; the other sailor was from Lysimachus' barge, which was from Mytilene.

The Tyrian sailor said to the sailor from Mytilene, "I am looking for Helicanus; he can give permission for your governor to come aboard. Oh, here he is."

He then said to Helicanus, "Sir, there's a barge that has come from Mytilene, and in it is Lysimachus the governor, who desires to come aboard. What is your will?"

"That he have his," Helicanus said. "Summon some gentlemen."

The Tyrian sailor shouted, "Ho, gentlemen! My lord calls."

Two or three gentlemen arrived.

The first gentleman asked, "Does your lordship call for us?"

"Gentlemen, there's some people of worth — members of the nobility — who want to come aboard. Please, greet them well."

The gentlemen and the two sailors left and went on board the barge.

Lysimachus and some lords exited the barge, along with the gentlemen and the two sailors.

The Tyrian sailor said to Lysimachus, indicating Helicanus, "Sir, this is the man who can answer all of your questions."

"Hail, reverend sir!" Lysimachus said. "May the gods preserve you!"

"And may the gods cause you, sir, to outlive the age I am, and die as I would die — honorably," Helicanus replied.

"You wish me well," Lysimachus said. "Being on shore, holding festivities in honor of the sea-god Neptune, and seeing this handsome vessel anchoring before us, I made my way to it, to know from where you came."

"First, what is your position?" Helicanus asked.

"I am the governor of this place you lie at anchor before — Mytilene."

"Sir, our vessel is from Tyre, and in it is King Pericles, who for the past three months has not spoken to anyone, nor has he taken sustenance except just enough to keep himself alive and prolong his grief."

"What is the reason for his malady?" Lysimachus asked.

"It would be too tedious to repeat, but his main grief springs from the loss of a beloved daughter and a wife."

"May we not see him?"

"You may, but seeing him will do no good," Helicanus said. "He will not speak to anyone."

"Yet let me obtain my wish," Lysimachus said.

"Here he is," Helicanus replied, walking Lysimachus and the others over to Pericles. "He was a handsome person, until the disaster that, one deadly night, drove him to this."

Pericles' misfortunes had started when he lost his wife; they had intensified when he was told that his daughter was dead.

"Sir King, all hail!" Lysimachus said. "May the gods preserve you! Hail, royal sir!"

"It is in vain," Helicanus said. "He will not speak to you."

The first lord said, "Sir, we have a maiden in Mytilene, whom I dare to wager would win some words from him. She can make him speak."

"That is a good idea," Lysimachus said, immediately realizing which maiden the first lord was referring to. "She with her sweet harmony of voice and with her other chosen attractions, would without question allure — win — him over. Just like soldiers forcing their way through a gateway, she would make a passage through his deafened parts, which now are halfway closed. She is the one who can make his half-deaf ears hear. She is most fortunate in being the most beautiful of all, and with her fellow maidens she is now upon the leafy shelter that abuts against the island's side."

The festivities honoring Neptune were taking place outside on the shore. A shelving — gently sloping — bank was on the side of the island, and it seemed to support the island. Some trees grew where the shelving bank met the island. Marina — the fairest maiden — and her female companions had seated themselves under those trees because their leaves provided shelter from the Sun.

Lysimachus ordered a lord to take the barge and get the fairest maiden. The lord exited.

Helicanus said, "To be sure, nothing has been effective in curing King Pericles, yet we'll do anything that might result in his recovery. But, since we have imposed on your kindness thus far, let us further ask you that in return for our gold we may have provisions. We need provisions not because we are destitute and lack money, but because we are weary of the staleness."

In this culture, keeping fresh food was difficult at sea. Canning had not yet been invented, and fresh fruits and vegetables had to be eaten quickly, as did non-preserved meat. Malnutrition was rampant among sailors, who often got the disease scurvy.

Lysimachus replied, "Sir, that is a courtesy that if we should deny it, the most just gods would send caterpillars to eat all the cultivated plants we have and so afflict our province with famine. Once again let me ask you to tell me — in more detail — the cause of your King's sorrow."

"Sit, sir. I will recount the story to you," Helicanus said.

He looked up and said, "But I see that I am prevented from doing so."

The lord had returned with the fairest maiden — Marina — who was accompanied by another young maiden who was carrying a harp.

"Oh, here is the lady whom I sent for," Lysimachus said. "Welcome, fair one!"

He asked Helicanus, "Isn't she attractive?"

"She's a gallant lady."

Lysimachus said, "She's such a lady, that, were I well assured that she was born into an aristocratic and noble family, I would wish no better choice to be my wife, and I would think myself extremely well wed."

He said to Marina, "Fair one, all goodness that consists in bounty expect even here, where is a Kingly patient who does not speak. You will be well rewarded if you can help this King. If your beneficial and skillful abilities can draw him out so that he speaks a few words in answer to you about anything, your sacred medicine shall receive such pay as your desires can wish."

"Sir, I will use my best skills in his recovery," Marina replied, "provided that none but I and my companion maiden are allowed to come near him."

"Come, let us leave her, and may the gods make her prosperous!" Lysimachus said.

He and the others withdrew from Pericles, Marina, and her maiden companion. They were not far away, but they did not look at Marina as she attempted to cure Pericles.

Marina sang, and her companion accompanied her on the harp.

Once the song had finished, Lysimachus came over and asked, "Did he pay any attention to your music?"

"No," Marina replied. "He did not even look at us."

Lysimachus went back to his companions and said, "Watch, she will speak to him."

"Hail, sir!" Marina said, going close to Pericles. "My lord, lend me an ear. Listen to me."

Pericles made a noise and pushed her away from him.

Marina said, "I am a maiden, my lord, who never before has invited eyes to look at me, but I have been gazed on as if I were a comet — something rare. I who am speaking, my lord, am one who, perhaps, has endured a grief that might equal yours, if both were justly and fairly weighed.

"Although wayward, capricious fortune has maligned and harmed me, I am descended from ancestors who were the equivalent of mighty Kings. But time has uprooted my parentage, and time has bound me in servitude to the world and to painful chance accidents."

Marina thought, *I will stop talking to him.*

She hesitated and thought, *But there is something inside me that causes my cheeks to glow and whispers in my ear, "Don't leave until he speaks."*

Pericles said, "'My fortunes' — 'parentage' — 'good parentage' — to equal mine! Was that what you said? What did you say?"

"I said, my lord, that if you knew my parentage, you would not do me violence," Marina said.

"I think you are right," Pericles replied. "Please, turn your eyes upon me."

A vision of his wife, Thaisa, began to fill his mind: "You are like something that — what country are you from? Are these shores where you were born?"

"No, nor was I born on any shores," replied Marina, who had been born at sea. "Yet I was mortally brought forth, and I am no other than I appear to be. I am a human being."

"I am great — pregnant — with woe, and I shall deliver tears with my weeping," Pericles said. "My dearest wife was like this maiden, and my daughter might have been such a one as this maiden. She has my Queen's high forehead. She has my wife's stature to an inch; her posture is as wand-like straight; she is as silver-voiced; her eyes are as jewel-like and are encased in eyebrows as beautiful. In her walk she is another Juno, Queen of the gods. And she starves the ears she feeds and makes them hungry the more she gives them speech — the more she speaks, the more her audience wants her to speak."

He said to Marina, "Where do you live?"

"Where I am only a stranger. From the deck you may see the place I live."

"Where were you raised? And how did you achieve these accomplishments, which you make richer because you have them?"

"If I should tell my history, it would seem like lies disdained in the reporting," Marina said. "You would not believe what I tell you."

"Please, speak," Pericles requested. "Falseness cannot come from you; you look as modest as Justice, and you seem to be a palace for the crowned Truth to dwell in. I will believe you, and I will make my senses believe you if you relate things that seem to be impossible because you look like someone I loved indeed.

"Who was your family?

"Didn't you say, when I pushed you away from me — which was when I first perceived you — that you came from good ancestors?"

"So indeed I did," Marina replied.

"Tell me your parentage. I think you said that you had been tossed from wrong to injury, and that you thought your griefs might equal mine, if both your griefs and mine were disclosed."

"Some such thing I said," Marina replied, "and I said no more but what I believe is likely to be true."

"Tell me your story," Pericles said. "If your griefs, carefully considered, prove to be one thousandth of the griefs that I have endured, then you are a man, and I have suffered like a girl — only a man could endure what I have endured and still live.

"Yet you look like a statue of Patience gazing on Kings' graves in a cemetery and smiling the most extreme calamities out of existence. One such as you would reject suicide.

"Who was your family? How did you lose them? What is your name, my most kind virgin?

"Tell me your story, I ask you. Come, sit by me."

"My name is Marina."

"Oh, I am being mocked," Pericles said. "Some angry god has sent you here to make the world laugh at me."

"Be calm, good sir, or I'll stop telling you my story."

"I'll be patient and calm," Pericles promised, "but you little know how much I was startled when you told me your name is Marina."

"The name was given to me by one who had some power: my father, who was a King."

"What!" Pericles said. "You are a King's daughter! And you are named Marina?"

"You said that you would believe me, but so that I am not a troubler of your peace, I will end my story here."

"But are you flesh and blood? Have you a working pulse? And are you no fairy?"

He felt her pulse and said, "Motion! I feel a pulse! Well; speak on. Where were you born? And why are you named Marina?"

"I was named Marina because I was born at sea."

"At sea! Who was your mother?"

"My mother was the daughter of a King; she died the minute I was born, as my good nurse, Lychorida, has often told me as she wept."

"Oh, stop there for a little while!" Pericles cried.

He thought, *This is the most excellent dream that dull sleep has ever mocked sad and distressed fools with. This maiden cannot be my daughter: My daughter's buried.*

He continued, "Well, where were you raised? I'll hear more, all the way to the bottom — the end — of your story, and I will never interrupt you."

"You are scornful of my story," Marina said. "Believe me, it is best that I stop telling it."

"I will believe every syllable of what you tell me. Still, let me ask these questions: How came you to live in these parts? Where were you raised?"

"The King my father left me in Tarsus until cruel Cleon, with his wicked wife, sought to murder me. They persuaded a villain to murder me, and after he had drawn his sword to do it, a crew of pirates came and rescued me. They brought me to Mytilene. But, good sir, where are your questions leading me?

Why do you weep? It may be that you think I am an impostor. No, indeed. I am the daughter of King Pericles, if good King Pericles is still alive."

"Helicanus!" Pericles shouted.

"Is my lord calling me?"

"You are a grave and noble counselor, very wise in many things. Tell me, if you can, who this maiden is, or what she is likely to be, who thus has made me weep?"

"I don't know, sir," Helicanus replied, "but here is the regent of Mytilene. He speaks nobly of her."

Lysimachus said, "She would never tell us her parentage. If we asked her to tell us, she would sit still and weep."

"Helicanus, hit me, honored sir," Pericles said. "Give me a gash and immediate pain lest this great sea of joys rushing upon me overpower the shores of my mortality and drown me with their sweetness."

He said to Marina, "Oh, come here, you have given birth to that man who begat you. You have given me a rebirth — you who were born at sea, buried at Tarsus, and found at sea again!"

He then said, "Helicanus, get down on your knees and thank the holy gods as loudly as thunder threatens us. This is Marina."

He asked her, "What was your mother's name? Tell me that because truth can never be confirmed enough even when all doubts sleep. I definitely know who you are, but please tell me this one additional detail."

"First, sir, let me ask you this: What is your title?"

"I am King Pericles of Tyre, but tell me now my drowned Queen's name. In all the rest that you have said, you have been as perfectly correct as a god would be, and you are the heir of Kingdoms and another life to me, Pericles, your father."

"All I have to do to be acknowledged as your daughter is to say my mother's name was Thaisa?" Marina asked. "Thaisa was my mother, whose life ended the minute mine began."

"Now I give you my blessing!" Pericles said. "Rise — you are my child."

He ordered an attendant, "Give me fresh garments."

Pericles was wearing dirty sackcloth in mourning; now he wanted his clean royal clothing.

He said, "She is my own daughter, Helicanus. She is not dead at Tarsus, although reports stated that savage Cleon killed her. She shall tell you everything, and you shall kneel, and acknowledge that she is your true Princess."

Looking at Lysimachus, he asked, "Who is this?"

Helicanus replied, "Sir, he is the governor of Mytilene, who, hearing of your melancholy and depressed state of mind, came to see you."

"I embrace you," Pericles said to Lysimachus, doing just that.

He ordered again, "Give me my royal robes. I am wild in my appearance."

He said, "May the Heavens bless my girl! But, listen. What music is that?"

He then said, "Tell Helicanus, my Marina, tell him what you have told me, point by point, for yet he seems to doubt that you are truly my daughter. But, what is that music?"

"My lord, I hear no music," Helicanus said.

"None!" Pericles said. "I hear the music of the spheres — the music of the planets and the stars as they move through the sky! Listen to it, my Marina."

"It is not good to contradict him," Lysimachus said. "Let him have his way."

"These are the rarest sounds! Don't you hear the music?" Pericles asked.

Humoring Pericles, Lysimachus said, "Yes, my lord, I hear it."

Music sounded. You, the reader, may hear it.

"This is most Heavenly music!" Pericles said. "It compels me to listen to it, and thick slumber hangs upon my eyes. Let me rest."

He began to sleep.

"Give him a pillow for his head," Lysimachus said. "Let all of us leave him. Well, my companion friends, if this but answer to my just belief, I'll well remember you."

Already, he was thinking of marrying Marina. He had just heard that she was the daughter of a King, and if so, she would be a good wife for him.

All except Pericles withdrew a short distance away, and the goddess Diana appeared to Pericles in a dream.

The goddess said to him, "My temple stands in Ephesus. Hurry there, and sacrifice upon my altar. There, when my chaste priests and nuns are met together, before all the people, reveal how you lost your wife at sea. To mourn your own sufferings, as well as your daughter's sufferings, recall them and speak about them accurately.

"Either perform my bidding, or you will live in woe. Do what I tell you to do, and you will be happy. I swear this by my silver bow!

"Awake, and tell everybody your dream."

The goddess disappeared.

Pericles woke up and said, "Celestial Diana, goddess argentine — goddess of silver — I will obey you."

He called, "Helicanus!"

Helicanus, Lysimachus, and Marina went to him.

"Sir?" Helicanus said.

Pericles said to Helicanus, "My plan was to sail for Tarsus, there to strike the inhospitable Cleon, but I have something else to do first. Turn our full sails toward Ephesus. Soon I'll tell you why."

He then said to Lysimachus, "Shall we refresh ourselves, sir, upon your shore, and I shall give you gold for such provisions as our plan will need?"

"Sir, with all my heart," Lysimachus said, "and, when you come ashore, I have another suit."

The first suit was Pericles' asking for provisions; Pericles was able to guess the second suit, which was Lysimachus'.

"You shall prevail if your suit is to woo my daughter, for it seems that you have nobly treated her."

"Sir, lend me your arm," Lysimachus said.

"Come, my Marina," Pericles said.

— 5.2 —

John Gower said to you, the reader, "Now our sands have almost run through the hourglass. Just a little more, and I will be silent. Please grant me this, my last request, because such kindness must relieve me.

"I want you to readily imagine with what pageantry, what feasts, what shows, and what minstrelsy and pretty sounds of celebration, the regent — Lysimachus — made in Mytilene to greet King Pericles. Lysimachus so thrived that he has been promised that fair Marina will be his wife. But this in no way will happen until King Pericles has made his sacrifice as the goddess Diana told him to do.

"Please make time pass quickly, and winged time fly. Now, winds fill sails, and things happen as our principals desire them to happen.

"So now imagine King Pericles and all his company at Ephesus, looking at the temple of Diana. That he can come here so soon is due to your imagination, for which I thank you."

At the temple of Diana in Ephesus, Thaisa — a high priestess — stood near the altar. A number of virgins were on each side of her. Also present were Cerimon and some attendants.

Pericles and his attendants entered the temple. Also with him were Lysimachus, Helicanus, Marina, and a lady.

Pericles said, "Hail, Diana! To perform your just command, I here confess myself the King of Tyre. I fled in fright from my country, and I wed at Pentapolis the fair Thaisa. She died at sea, but first she gave birth to a girl named Marina, who, goddess, still wears your silver livery — she is still a virgin. She at Tarsus was raised as a member of Cleon's family, but when she was fourteen years old, he sought to murder her. A better fortune brought her to Mytilene. My ship anchored by that country's shore, and her fortunes brought the maiden aboard, where, by her own very clear memory of past events, she made known to me that she is my daughter."

After hearing his voice, a shocked Thaisa looked at Pericles, although as a priestess, she was not supposed to. She said, "Voice and appearance! You are, you are — oh, royal Pericles!"

She fainted.

"What does the nun mean?" Pericles asked.

Thaisa was wearing a veil, so Pericles did not recognize her.

He said, "She is dying! Help, gentlemen!"

Cerimon quickly went to Thaisa's side, and immediately knew that she had only fainted and would quickly recover.

He said to Pericles, "Noble sir, if what you have said before Diana's altar is true, this is your wife."

"Reverend sir, no," Pericles replied. "I threw my wife's body overboard with these very arms."

"You did that when you were near this coast, I am sure," Cerimon said.

"That is most certainly true," Pericles replied.

"Look after the lady," Cerimon said to some attendants.

He then said, "She has fainted from an excess of joy. Early on a blustery morning, this lady was thrown upon this shore. I opened her coffin, found rich jewels inside, revived her, and placed her here in Diana's temple."

"May we see the jewels?" Pericles asked.

The jewels would confirm Thaisa's identity.

"Great sir, they shall be brought to you at my house, where I invite you — look, Thaisa is recovering."

"Oh, let me look at him!" Thaisa said, aware that as a priestess of the virgin goddess Diana, normally she would not look at a man. "If he is not my husband, then my position as holy priestess will not allow me to feel any sexual desire for him. If he is not my husband, then my position as holy priestess will curb my sexual desire, no matter what I see."

She looked at Pericles and said, "Oh, my lord, aren't you Pericles? You spoke like him; you look like him. Didn't you mention a tempest, a birth, and a death?"

"It is the voice of dead Thaisa!" Pericles said.

"I am Thaisa, whom you supposed to be dead and drowned."

"Immortal Diana!" Pericles said.

"Now I know you better," Thaisa said. "When we with tears departed from Pentapolis, my father the King — Simonides — gave you a ring like this."

She showed him a ring that she was wearing. Pericles immediately recognized it.

"This ... this ... no more, you gods!" he said. His happiness filled him; he had no room for more.

He continued, "Gods, your present kindness makes my past miseries mere entertainments. You shall do well, if once I touch her lips I melt and am seen no more. I shall die of happiness."

He said to Thaisa, "Oh, come, and be buried a second time within these arms."

They hugged.

Marina said, "My heart leaps to go into my mother's bosom."

She knelt.

"Look at who is kneeling here!" Pericles said. "She is flesh of your flesh, Thaisa. You gave birth to her at sea, and she was named Marina because she was born at sea."

"We are blest — she is my own!" Thaisa said. She raised Marina up from her kneeling position and hugged her.

"Hail, madam, and my Queen!" Helicanus said.

"I don't know you," Thaisa said to him. She had never met him.

"You have heard me say that when I fled away from Tyre, I left behind an old man to rule as my substitute," Pericles said. "Can you remember what I called the man? I have often said his name."

"Helicanus," Thaisa said.

"This is still more confirmation that you are my wife," Pericles said. "Embrace him, dear Thaisa; this is he."

Thaisa and Helicanus hugged.

Pericles said to Thaisa, "Now I long to hear how you were found, how your life could possibly be preserved; and whom to thank, besides the gods, for this great miracle."

"You can thank Lord Cerimon, my lord," Thaisa replied. "Lord Cerimon, through whom the gods have shown their power, is the man who can from first to last answer your questions."

Pericles said to Cerimon, "Reverend sir, the gods can have no mortal officer more like a god than you. Will you tell me how this once-dead Queen lives again?"

"I will, my lord," Cerimon said. "But please, first go with me to my house, where you shall be shown everything that was found with her in the coffin. I will tell you how she came to be placed here in the temple. I will omit no important information."

Pericles prayed, "Pure and chaste Diana, bless you for your vision! I will offer night devotions to you."

He then said, "Thaisa, this Prince, Lysimachus, the fair-betrothed of your daughter, shall marry her at Pentapolis. And now, this ornament — my shaggy hair and beard — that makes me look unkempt and dismal I will clip so that I have a respectable haircut."

He said to Marina, "What no razor has touched for fourteen years, I'll beautify to grace your marriage-day."

Thaisa said, "Lord Cerimon has credible letters, sir, that say my father, Simonides, is dead."

"May the Heavens make a star of him and put him in the firmament! Yet there in Pentapolis, his Kingdom, my Queen, we'll celebrate Lysimachus and Marina's nuptials, and we ourselves will in that Kingdom spend our following days. Our son-in-law and daughter shall reign in Tyre."

He then said, "Lord Cerimon, we have been putting off our desire to hear the rest of the story. Sir, lead us to your house."

— Epilogue —

John Gower said to you, the reader, "You have seen Antiochus and his daughter, who engaged in monstrous and incestuous lust, receive their due and just reward.

"Pericles, his Queen, and his daughter, as you have seen, although they were assailed with fortune fierce and keen, preserved their virtue from deadly destruction's blast. Heaven led them, and they were crowned with joy at last.

"In Helicanus you have seen a figure of truth, of faith, and of loyalty.

"In reverend Cerimon there well appears the worth that learned charity always wears.

"After news had spread of the cursed deed of wicked Cleon and his wife, who wanted to murder Marina, the citizens — because of the honored name of Pericles, who had delivered grain to them when they were famished — raged throughout the city and burned Cleon and his wife in his palace. The gods seemed content to punish them for the crime of murder, although the murder was not done, but only meant.

"So, to thank you for your patience in reading this, may you find new joy! Here our book has its ending."

Appendix A: About the Author

It was a dark and stormy night. Suddenly a cry rang out, and on a hot summer night in 1954, Josephine, wife of Carl Bruce, gave birth to a boy — me. Unfortunately, this young married couple allowed Reuben Saturday, Josephine's brother, to name their first-born. Reuben, aka "The Joker," decided that Bruce was a nice name, so he decided to name me Bruce Bruce. I have gone by my middle name — David — ever since.

Being named Bruce David Bruce hasn't been all bad. Bank tellers remember me very quickly, so I don't often have to show an ID. It can be fun in charades, also. When I was a counselor as a teenager at Camp Echoing Hills in Warsaw, Ohio, a fellow counselor gave the signs for "sounds like" and "two words," then she pointed to a bruise on her leg twice. Bruise Bruise? Oh yeah, Bruce Bruce is the answer!

Uncle Reuben, by the way, gave me a haircut when I was in kindergarten. He cut my hair short and shaved a small bald spot on the back of my head. My mother wouldn't let me go to school until the bald spot grew out again.

Of all my brothers and sisters (six in all), I am the only transplant to Athens, Ohio. I was born in Newark, Ohio, and have lived all around Southeastern Ohio. However, I moved to Athens to go to Ohio University and have never left.

At Ohio U, I never could make up my mind whether to major in English or Philosophy, so I got a bachelor's degree with a double major in both areas, then I added a master's degree in English and a master's degree in Philosophy.

Currently, and for a long time to come (I eat fruits and vegetables), I am spending my retirement writing books such as *Nadia Comaneci: Perfect 10*, *The Funniest People in Dance*, *Homer's* Iliad: *A Retelling in Prose*, and *William Shakespeare's* Othello: *A Retelling in Prose*.

By the way, my sister Brenda Kennedy writes romances such as *A New Beginning* and *Shattered Dreams*.

Appendix B: Some Books by David Bruce

Retellings of a Classic Work of Literature

Arden of Faversham: *A Retelling*

Ben Jonson's The Alchemist: *A Retelling*

Ben Jonson's The Arraignment, or Poetaster: *A Retelling*

Ben Jonson's Bartholomew Fair: *A Retelling*

Ben Jonson's The Case is Altered: *A Retelling*

Ben Jonson's Catiline's Conspiracy: *A Retelling*

Ben Jonson's The Devil is an Ass: *A Retelling*

Ben Jonson's Epicene: *A Retelling*

Ben Jonson's Every Man in His Humor: *A Retelling*

Ben Jonson's Every Man Out of His Humor: *A Retelling*

Ben Jonson's The Fountain of Self-Love, or Cynthia's Revels: *A Retelling*

Ben Jonson's The Magnetic Lady, or Humors Reconciled: *A Retelling*

Ben Jonson's The New Inn, or The Light Heart: *A Retelling*

Ben Jonson's Sejanus' Fall: *A Retelling*

Ben Jonson's The Staple of News: *A Retelling*

Ben Jonson's A Tale of a Tub: *A Retelling*

Ben Jonson's Volpone, or the Fox: *A Retelling*

Christopher Marlowe's Complete Plays: Retellings

Christopher Marlowe's Dido, Queen of Carthage: *A Retelling*

Christopher Marlowe's Doctor Faustus: *Retellings of the 1604 A-Text and of the 1616 B-Text*

Christopher Marlowe's Edward II: *A Retelling*

Christopher Marlowe's The Massacre at Paris: *A Retelling*

Christopher Marlowe's The Rich Jew of Malta: *A Retelling*

Christopher Marlowe's Tamburlaine, Parts 1 and 2: *Retellings*

Dante's Divine Comedy: *A Retelling in Prose*

Dante's Inferno: *A Retelling in Prose*

Dante's Purgatory: *A Retelling in Prose*

Dante's Paradise: *A Retelling in Prose*

The Famous Victories of Henry V: *A Retelling*

From the Iliad *to the* Odyssey: *A Retelling in Prose of Quintus of Smyrna's* Posthomerica

George Chapman, Ben Jonson, and John Marston's Eastward Ho! *A Retelling*

George Peele's The Arraignment of Paris: *A Retelling*

George Peele's The Battle of Alcazar: *A Retelling*

George Peele's David and Bathsheba, and the Tragedy of Absalom: *A Retelling*

George Peele's Edward I: *A Retelling*

George Peele's The Old Wives' Tale: *A Retelling*

George-a-Greene: *A Retelling*

The History of King Leir: *A Retelling*

Homer's Iliad: *A Retelling in Prose*

Homer's Odyssey: *A Retelling in Prose*

J.W. Gent.'s The Valiant Scot: *A Retellings*

Jason and the Argonauts: A Retelling in Prose of Apollonius of Rhodes' Argonautica

John Ford: Eight Plays Translated into Modern English

John Ford's The Broken Heart: *A Retelling*

John Ford's The Fancies, Chaste and Noble: *A Retelling*

John Ford's The Lady's Trial: *A Retelling*

John Ford's The Lover's Melancholy: *A Retelling*

John Ford's Love's Sacrifice: *A Retelling*

John Ford's Perkin Warbeck: *A Retelling*

John Ford's The Queen: *A Retelling*

John Ford's 'Tis Pity She's a Whore: *A Retelling*

John Lyly's Campaspe: *A Retelling*

John Lyly's Endymion, The Man in the Moon: *A Retelling*

John Lyly's Galatea: *A Retelling*

John Lyly's Love's Metamorphosis: *A Retelling*

John Lyly's Midas: *A Retelling*

John Lyly's Mother Bombie: *A Retelling*

John Lyly's Sappho and Phao: *A Retelling*

John Lyly's The Woman in the Moon: *A Retelling*

John Webster's The White Devil: *A Retelling*

King Edward III: *A Retelling*

Mankind: *A Medieval Morality Play* (A Retelling)

Margaret Cavendish's The Unnatural Tragedy: *A Retelling*

The Merry Devil of Edmonton: *A Retelling*

The Summoning of Everyman: *A Medieval Morality Play* (A Retelling)

Robert Greene's Friar Bacon and Friar Bungay: *A Retelling*

The Taming of a Shrew: *A Retelling*

Tarlton's Jests: A Retelling

Thomas Middleton's A Chaste Maid in Cheapside: *A Retelling*

Thomas Middleton's Women Beware Women: *A Retelling*

Thomas Middleton and Thomas Dekker's The Roaring Girl: *A Retelling*

Thomas Middleton and William Rowley's The Changeling: *A Retelling*

The Trojan War and Its Aftermath: Four Ancient Epic Poems

Virgil's Aeneid: *A Retelling in Prose*

William Shakespeare's 5 Late Romances: Retellings in Prose

William Shakespeare's 10 Histories: Retellings in Prose

William Shakespeare's 11 Tragedies: Retellings in Prose

William Shakespeare's 12 Comedies: Retellings in Prose

William Shakespeare's 38 Plays: Retellings in Prose

William Shakespeare's 1 Henry IV, aka Henry IV, Part 1: *A Retelling in Prose*

William Shakespeare's 2 Henry IV, aka Henry IV, Part 2: *A Retelling in Prose*

William Shakespeare's 1 Henry VI, aka Henry VI, Part 1: *A Retelling in Prose*

William Shakespeare's 2 Henry VI, aka Henry VI, Part 2: *A Retelling in Prose*

William Shakespeare's 3 Henry VI, aka Henry VI, Part 3: *A Retelling in Prose*

William Shakespeare's All's Well that Ends Well: *A Retelling in Prose*

William Shakespeare's Antony and Cleopatra: *A Retelling in Prose*

William Shakespeare's As You Like It: *A Retelling in Prose*

William Shakespeare's The Comedy of Errors: *A Retelling in Prose*

William Shakespeare's Coriolanus: *A Retelling in Prose*

William Shakespeare's Cymbeline: *A Retelling in Prose*

William Shakespeare's Hamlet: *A Retelling in Prose*

William Shakespeare's Henry V: *A Retelling in Prose*

William Shakespeare's Henry VIII: *A Retelling in Prose*

William Shakespeare's Julius Caesar: *A Retelling in Prose*

William Shakespeare's King John: *A Retelling in Prose*

William Shakespeare's King Lear: *A Retelling in Prose*

William Shakespeare's Love's Labor's Lost: *A Retelling in Prose*

William Shakespeare's Macbeth: *A Retelling in Prose*

William Shakespeare's Measure for Measure: *A Retelling in Prose*

William Shakespeare's The Merchant of Venice: *A Retelling in Prose*

William Shakespeare's The Merry Wives of Windsor: *A Retelling in Prose*

William Shakespeare's A Midsummer Night's Dream: *A Retelling in Prose*

William Shakespeare's Much Ado About Nothing: *A Retelling in Prose*

William Shakespeare's Othello: *A Retelling in Prose*

William Shakespeare's Pericles, Prince of Tyre: *A Retelling in Prose*

William Shakespeare's Richard II: *A Retelling in Prose*

William Shakespeare's Richard III: *A Retelling in Prose*

William Shakespeare's Romeo and Juliet: *A Retelling in Prose*

William Shakespeare's The Taming of the Shrew: *A Retelling in Prose*

William Shakespeare's The Tempest: *A Retelling in Prose*

William Shakespeare's Timon of Athens: *A Retelling in Prose*

William Shakespeare's Titus Andronicus: *A Retelling in Prose*

William Shakespeare's Troilus and Cressida: *A Retelling in Prose*

William Shakespeare's Twelfth Night: *A Retelling in Prose*

William Shakespeare's The Two Gentlemen of Verona: *A Retelling in Prose*

William Shakespeare's The Two Noble Kinsmen: *A Retelling in Prose*

William Shakespeare's The Winter's Tale: *A Retelling in Prose*